TOO GOOD TO BE TRUE

Later that night, long after the boys had gone home, Marty snuggled beneath an old-fashioned quilt and whispered to Brenda, "Who's Lila?"

The springs squeaked as Brenda turned over in the bunk above her. "She's a girl Hank's been dating."

Marty groaned and covered her ears with her pillow. *Forget it, he's taken!* she told herself. But when she closed her eyes, all she could think about was Hank kissing her. In another split second, she would have been kissing him back. What would have happened then?

Bantam Sweet Dreams romances
Ask your bookseller for the books you have missed

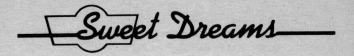

TOO GOOD
TO
BE TRUE

Susan Kirby

BANTAM BOOKS
NEW YORK • TORONTO • LONDON • SYDNEY • AUCKLAND

RL 6, age 11 and up

TOO GOOD TO BE TRUE

A Bantam Book / October 1991

ISBN 0-553-29213-7

Published simultaneously in the United States and Canada

Bantam Books are published by Bantam Books, a division
of Bantam Doubleday Dell Publishing Group, Inc. Its trademark, consisting of the words "Bantam Books" and the
portrayal of a rooster, is Registered in U.S. Patent and
Trademark Office and in other countries. Marca Regis-
trada. Bantam Books, 666 Fifth Avenue, New York, New
York 10103.

PRINTED IN THE UNITED STATES OF AMERICA

OPM   0   9   8   7   6   5   4   3   2   1

To Mike, Debbie,
Betsy, Katie, and Jonathan
for keepin'
life sweet at the Grove

Chapter One

"Ask for Sally," Marty Evans said as she and her best friend, Brenda Kelly, stopped in front of Regis Hair Salon.

Brenda hung back. "I'm not so sure about this."

"It's just a trim."

"Yeah—remind me of that forty minutes from now when I come out looking like I tangled with a runaway weed whacker!"

Marty giggled. "Relax, Bren. Sally's good, I promise."

Brenda studied Marty's shoulder-length blond hair. "She does a super job on you. Guess I'll give it a shot. Go buy your sneakers, then meet me at Garcia's Pizza. I'll cheat on my diet and buy you a slice. Unless Sally

1

ruins my hair, in which case I'll call off my date with Scott and drown you in a water pitcher."

"I thought you were going out with Roger tonight," Marty said.

"No, that's not until next month. He's got tickets to see Phantom Spry. Hey, do you and Darrin want to double?"

"Sounds like fun. I'll mention it to Darrin." But as Marty started walking through the mall, she wasn't sure that Darrin would want to go. He did the same thing every weekend. Darrin was a pretty predictable guy. Marty let out a little sigh. A rock concert *would* be a nice change. . . .

On impulse, Marty stopped by Ticketron. There were still tickets available for the Phantom Spry concert, so she hurried to a pay phone and punched in Darrin's number.

Darrin wasn't home, but Marty thought she should buy the tickets anyway and make it her treat. She hesitated, thinking it over. The concert was on a Friday night, and Darrin always spent Friday nights hanging out with his friends. If he wasn't interested in the concert, she wouldn't get to see Phantom Spry and she'd be broke besides! Finally, Marty decided to shop for her sneakers, then try Darrin's number again.

At the Foot Locker, Marty pointed out pale-pink high-tops to the salesclerk, then waited for him to return with a pair in her size. Marty fluffed her hair out over the collar of her pale blue ski jacket and thought about how great the sneakers were going to look with her stone-washed jeans. Just then two boys wearing Woodland Grove High jackets came into the store and paused at a rack of sweatpants. The taller of the two turned to a display of sleeveless track shirts. Something about him was vaguely familiar. Marty stole another glimpse as the boy peeled off his coat. He was pulling a red jersey on over his T-shirt when his gaze met Marty's. A smile tugged at his mouth.

Marty's pulse quickened. He had nice brown eyes! She noticed the length of his lashes, too, and the casual way his sandy hair fell across his forehead. Where had she seen him before?

"Here you go, Miss."

Marty turned to the salesman and slipped out of her white sneakers. He pulled a pink high-top out of the box and loosened the laces. Marty put one shoe on and stood to get the feel of it. "They seem a little tight."

"Who'd guess a little thing like you'd have . . ." The middle-aged clerk flushed and didn't finish his remark.

"Big feet?" Marty finished. She held out

3

her feet and wiggled her toes. "My father teases me about them all the time. They hold me up, so I guess I can't complain."

Marty heard him chuckle to himself as he started toward the storeroom to exchange the shoes for a larger pair. Waiting for the clerk to return, Marty glanced at the dark-eyed boy again. Woodland Grove was a fierce football rival of her school, Riverton High. But even if he was on the team, there was no reason she should recognize him. And yet, she couldn't shake the feeling she'd seen him before.

The boy pulled on a hooded sweatshirt and moved toward the full-length mirror directly in front of Marty.

"Excuse me," he said as he passed in front of her.

Marty watched him in the mirror. His shoulders were broad beneath the soft fleece of the sweatshirt. When he shrugged, the sweatshirt rode up to reveal a hand-tooled leather belt. The name "Hank" was slashed by a faded-denim belt loop. Hank. She didn't know anybody named Hank, did she? It was driving her crazy that she couldn't place him!

His friend shifted from foot to foot and drummed his fingers on a shoe box. "Why don't you get your shoes here, too?"

"Low cash flow. They'll have to wait a

week." Hank glanced at his friend before tugging the sweatshirt up over his head. "Sure I can't talk you into going out for track, Orin? You could throw the shot," he added, his words muffled by the fleece.

"Yeah, like I'm going to hustle around that track doing laps just for the fun of it. Pick on someone else, man!" Short and stocky with stubbled cheeks, Orin gave Hank a playful shove. Hank's head was still buried in the sweatshirt and he stumbled and came down hard on the tips of Marty's toes. She winced and drew her foot back as he pulled off the shirt.

"Oops! Hey, I'm sorry!"

Resisting the urge to clutch her toes, Marty held back a grimace. "That's okay."

"Are you sure?"

He was looking into her face with such earnest concern that Marty's heart skipped a beat. Heat rushed up her neck and into her cheeks and she said flippantly, "I guess I can forget ballet. But other than that . . ."

He looked even more distressed. "You're a dancer?"

Marty laughed and shook her head. "No, I was just kidding."

"Then I'm off the hook?" At her nod, he slapped his hand over his heart and let out a sigh of relief.

Responding to the sparkle in his eye, Marty laughed again. But before she could say anything else, the clerk returned with another pair of shoes and Hank walked over to the cashier to make his purchases.

"These should do the trick," the salesclerk said as Marty poked her foot into one shoe. He tightened the laces and tied a firm bow. "There. How does that feel?"

"Pretty good."

"Let's put the other one on, then you can try them out," the clerk suggested.

Marty tested the shoes, walking toward the front of the store. Hank was following his friend out the door when he suddenly turned and caught Marty looking after him. He grinned, lifted a hand and called over his shoulder, "See you." Marty smiled and returned his wave.

When she'd paid for her shoes, Marty tried Darrin's number again, but he still wasn't home. She went on to Garcia's and ordered sodas and two slices. The pizza arrived at the table just as Brenda sailed through the door.

Marty nudged a chair out from the table for her friend. "Perfect timing! And your hair looks great!"

"You're right. Sally's good. Am I beautiful, or what?"

Brenda ran bright-colored nails through

her dark, glossy hair. She struck a pose and batted her eyelashes.

Marty laughed. "And modest, too. Seriously, you do look terrific. It makes your eyes look bigger, too."

"And my wallet smaller. The money I earned bottling maple syrup out at Gram's is going fast. Oh well, I'm worth it." Brenda eyed the pizza. "I'm glad you ordered. I'm starved!"

Marty caught a string of melting cheese with her finger and wrapped it back neatly over her slice of pizza. "I wish you'd been at the shoe store. There were two guys there, and one of them looked familiar. But I just couldn't place him."

Brenda's green eyes sparkled with interest. "And here I thought you had eyes only for Darrin."

Marty shrugged. "My eyes occasionally stray. No harm in looking, you know."

"So what did these straying eyes of yours see?"

"Well, he was about average height and broad-shouldered. He had sandy-colored hair and his eyes were a nice shade of brown. He was kind of a hunk, to be honest."

"Wow! Did you talk to him?" Brenda asked eagerly.

"Just a few words." Between bites of pizza,

Marty told her all about it, adding, "Not that I'll ever see him again." Then Marty went on to tell Brenda about the Phantom Spry tickets.

"Buy them," Brenda said.

"But what if Darrin doesn't want to go?"

"*You* want to go, don't you?"

"Yes, but . . ."

"Then buy them. If Darrin doesn't want to go, find someone who does. That shouldn't be too hard. Phantom Spry is hot!"

Take another guy? Marty opened her mouth to protest, then closed it again. Brenda dated a lot of different boys, and Marty wasn't sure she could make her understand the loyalty and affection she felt for Darrin. Darrin was good-looking, well-mannered, and he treated her as an equal, which was more than she could say for some of the guys she'd dated. Not that Darrin was perfect. Marty sometimes wished he could be a little more spontaneous and less predictable. But Marty was reluctant to admit that her relationship with Darrin wasn't absolutely ideal.

When they'd finished eating, Marty tried Darrin's number a third time. Again, no luck. So, with a little prodding from Brenda, Marty bought the Phantom Spry tickets anyway.

Chapter Two

The Evanses' two-story white house on Gridley Street sat midblock between Mr. Coltry's bungalow on the north and the Kellys' sprawling brick house on the south. Brenda pulled her car into the driveway of the brick house and shut off the engine. "Can you come in for a while?" she asked.

Marty shook her head. "I promised to do a few chores as soon as I got home."

"Both of your parents are at the store?"

"They're having a two-for-one sale on reclining chairs. Mom thought she might need Dad's help," Marty said. Her father, a newspaper columnist, often pitched in at the furniture store her mother owned and operated. "You could come keep me company, though."

"Sorry, I've got a whole stack of paper bags to slit for Gram. My cousin's supposed to stop by and pick them up this afternoon."

"Give me a few minutes to wash the dishes and fix the plug on D.C.'s lamp, and I'll help you," Marty offered.

"Okay, I'll bring the bags over."

Brenda ran into her house and Marty crossed to her own yard, dodging dirty patches of snow. As she let herself in the back door, her black cat, D.C., slipped out. "D.C., you come back here, or we'll both be in hot water!" she warned. Marty had found the cat on her doorstep upon returning from a family vacation to Washington, D.C., a few years earlier.

D.C. paid no attention to her. Sighing, Marty closed the screen door that led from the garage to the kitchen and went inside. After she took off her jacket, she opened a can of cat food and filled D.C.'s dish.

"D.C.? Here, kitty, kitty, kitty," she called outside.

The cat scrambled out of Mr. Coltry's oak tree and bolted across the yard toward Marty. She placed D.C.'s dish on the garage floor next to the padded wooden box where he slept. A heat lamp hung over his box to keep him warm on cold nights.

"Been bird-watching again? Mr. Coltry'll have a fit if he catches you in his tree," she scolded.

D.C. twitched one ear and went right on eating. Marty freshened his water, then rummaged through a drawer to find tools to replace the faulty plug on the end of D.C.'s heat lamp cord.

As she glanced toward the back door, Marty saw Brenda staggering beneath a pile of brown paper grocery bags.

Marty opened the door and grabbed a handful just before they hit the floor. "What's your grandmother going to do with all these bags?" she asked.

"She uses them for wrapping mail orders out at the syrup camp," Brenda told her, dropping the rest of the bags on the kitchen table.

"You can buy brown paper on a roll, can't you?"

"Sure. But Gram's got a thing about recycling. Figures she's saving a tree or two." Brenda fished two pairs of scissors out of her coat pocket, then flung her coat over the back of a chair and sat down. "It's easy to do. Just cut the bottom out and slit down one side, like this." As she demonstrated, Brenda glanced over at the tools on the counter. "What were you up to—major surgery?"

"Like I said, I was going to fix the plug on D.C.'s heat lamp. The wires are starting to fray," Marty told her.

11

The girls started to work nearly as fast as they talked. They were making good headway on the bags when Brenda cocked her head to one side and listened.

"Is someone at the door?"

Marty listened a moment too, then sighed. "It's D.C. He climbs up the screen and makes the door rattle like that." She got out of her chair and opened the inside door. Halfway up the screen, D.C. peered through the wire mesh and blinked his big green eyes. "You get down from there, I mean it!"

D.C. let go of the screen and jumped down. Marty closed the inside door, muttering, "I should have named him 'Trouble'. He's always in it! Mr. Coltry's always complaining about him, plus there's Dad's allergies. Not to mention that Dad's ticked off over the screen door. He just replaced it last fall and he's threatened to get rid of D.C. if he has to replace it again. I've tried everything to stop that silly cat from climbing it, even throwing water on him."

"He's just being sociable. Why don't you let him in?" Brenda suggested.

"Dad would sneeze his head off. He'd know in a minute that D.C.'s been in here. Cut it out, D.C., or I'm going to give you a shower!" Marty yelled as the screen banged again.

But the cat kept it up, and Marty finally

made good on her threat, filling a glass with water and sloshing it through the mesh. In case D.C. didn't get the message, she refilled the glass and left it on the counter near the door.

The girls were halfway through the stack of bags when the rapping at the door began again. Marty slipped out of her chair and tiptoed to the door. "This time he's really going to get it! You open the door and I'll be ready with the water," she whispered to Brenda.

"Okay." Brenda put her hand on the doorknob and whispered, "Ready?"

Marty nodded. As Brenda jerked open the door, Marty flung the water at the middle of the screen.

Marty froze in her tracks, noticing a startled boy standing on the other side of the screen.

It couldn't be! She blinked, but the sandy-haired boy from the shoe store did not disappear. He just stood there with water dripping from his nose, his chin, and his gold-tipped lashes. Marty stared at him in dismay.

"I thought you were D.C.!"

"I'm glad I'm not, if that's the welcome he gets!" Hank said, drying his face with the sleeve of his jacket.

Behind Marty, Brenda burst into laughter,

and Marty shot her a withering glance. Face flaming, she grabbed a dish towel. "I'm so sorry! Come in—here's a towel—I'm so sorry," she babbled, adding with a hiss, "Bren, *stop it*! It isn't funny!"

Hank looked from Brenda to Marty, who was propping the screen door open with her foot and holding out the towel. His bewildered expression added to Marty's embarrassment and confusion, but Brenda went right on laughing. When she was finally able to speak, she cried, "That's my *cousin*!" Brenda grabbed the towel from Marty's hand and patted her eyes dry. "Hank, meet Marty Evans. Marty, this is my cousin, Harold Maxwell."

Hank brushed a trickle of water off his chin, staring at Marty. "Didn't I see you at the Foot Locker today?"

Marty nodded and started apologizing again. "I can't tell you how sorry I am!" She went on to explain about the cat. "It's safe to come in now, Harold, honest!"

He grinned. "Call me Hank. Everybody does except my dimwit cousin."

"Harold's a perfectly respectable name," Brenda said with a twinkle in her eye.

Hank snatched the towel away from Brenda, dried the front of his coat, then snapped the towel at his cousin. "That's for calling me *Harold*!" He snapped it again. "And *that's* for laughing!"

Brenda scooted out of his way. "I couldn't help it, Hank. You looked so *funny*! I don't know who was more surprised—you or Marty. Did Mom send you over for the bags?"

Hank nodded and glanced at the table. "Doesn't look like you're done, though."

Brenda shoved a pair of scissors into Hank's hand and pulled out a chair. "You might as well help us finish. Marty, can you find another pair of scissors?"

"Why don't I just take the ones you've done?" Hank suggested.

"What's your hurry?" Brenda asked.

"Orin's waiting in the car," he told her.

Brenda smiled. "Great! He can help, too. Go out there and tell him I said so."

Hank shrugged and headed for the door. "Okay. Be right back." He slid Marty a glance and added belatedly, "If it's all right with you, that is."

"Sure, bring him in," Marty said. Once he was out of sight, she whispered to Brenda, "The Kelly family reunion! *That's* where I met him!"

"Hey, that's right. You were over my house when we had it last year. So you two *have* met. I wonder if Hank remembers?"

Hank soon returned with his friend. Brenda already knew Orin, so Hank introduced him to Marty.

"Didn't Hank and I see you in the Foot Locker today?" Orin asked, looking at her closely.

Hank chuckled. "Yeah, we did. But that was before I knew what a wicked left arm this girl's got."

The boys sat down at the table and started helping Marty and Brenda slit the rest of the bags. They finished in no time, and the boys stood up to leave.

"Gram's probably wondering what's keeping me," Hank said, giving half the bags to Orin.

Orin swung out the door and D.C. slipped in. Marty dived for him, explaining to Hank, "He has to stay out. Dad's allergic to cat fur."

But D.C. played catch-me-if-you-can, and Hank joined Marty in the chase. Marty lunged for the cat, but he glided past her, then sat down under the table just out of reach. Marty got down on her hands and knees, calling, "Here, D.C. Here, kitty!"

Green eyes narrowed, D.C. shot toward the pantry, making a wide path around Hank. Marty sat back on her heels and groaned in defeat.

She sighed. "Never mind—just let him go. The more you chase him, the faster he runs.

He'll calm down in a minute and come out of hiding."

"Okay," Hank said.

Then suddenly Marty's tongue felt thick, and the silence grew awkward. Leaping to her feet, she gathered up her tools and a length of new electrical cord.

"Don't tell me—you're going to shock him out of hiding, right?" Hank said, grinning.

His joke broke the tension, and they both laughed. Marty explained about the frayed wires on the heat lamp cord, and the next thing she knew, Hank was out in the garage, snipping off the old cord and replacing it with the new one.

A little miffed that he obviously thought a chore like that was "man's work," Marty thanked Hank politely and waved as he hurried across the lawn to Brenda's driveway where Orin and Brenda were leaning against a beat-up old truck.

A few minutes later, Marty heard the truck roar to life and Brenda came across the yard. "Orin's kind of cute, don't you think?" she asked as she came inside.

"He's okay," Marty murmured.

"You and *Harold* seemed to hit it off. Isn't my cousin a hunk?" Brenda teased.

Marty grinned. "A 'Hank,' at least!"

"Both Orin and Hank will be working out

at the syrup camp. The season doesn't last long—eight weeks at the most. But eight weeks is plenty of time to make some headway, if you know what I mean," Brenda teased.

"Headway in what?" Marty asked innocently.

Brenda shot her a wicked grin. "Do I have to draw you a picture, or what?" She laughed at Marty's blush. "I know, I know—you're spoken for. Still, Gram can always use a little extra help, and I could use the company. Why don't you come along with me next Saturday? It'll be fun, I promise!"

Chapter Three

On Saturday morning, Marty put on a white cable-knit sweater and new pale-blue ski pants. She paused to look at herself in the mirror. Warm and stylish, too, she thought.

Marty closed the door to her messy room and hurried downstairs. Her mother looked up from the inventory sheet she was scanning and raised her eyebrows. "Pretty fancy for working at a maple syrup camp. Wouldn't an old coat and a couple of layers of jeans be more suitable?"

Marty rolled her eyes. "Mom, there's nothing more uncool than three layers of clothes!"

Marty's mother looked amused. "I didn't realize this was a fashion show. What about a hat and gloves? Are they out of style, too?"

Marty patted the bulging pocket of her ski jacket. "Got them right here."

"Good girl." Her mother glanced at her wristwatch. "I'd better get going in a few minutes, too. If you think of it, bring home a bottle of syrup and we'll talk your father into fixing waffles for breakfast tomorrow," she added, following Marty to the door.

"Sounds great. I won't forget," Marty promised.

It was a thirty-minute ride out to Brenda's grandparents' place, but the drive passed quickly. Light snow had fallen the previous night and brightened the woodlands surrounding Sugar Creek Maple Camp. Brenda parked her car at the end of a short winding lane and pointed to the steam billowing from the little cupola atop the sugar house.

"Looks like Grandpa Kelly's getting an early start," she said. "Weekends are always busy—people like to wander in and look around while he's cooking. By midafternoon, we'll be tripping over tourists."

Marty stepped out of the car and took a deep breath. The air was sharp and cold and faintly maple-scented. "Mmm, smells good."

"Sweet, too. One thousand calories per breath," Brenda joked. "But who's counting?"

Marty grinned at her weight-conscious

friend and took a good look around. Oddly enough, she had never been here before. The sugar house with the salesroom at one end of it was painted the same dark red as the rambling farmhouse. In the background she could see a barn and several smaller out-buildings. Timberland encircled the clearing on three sides, and the snow-covered trees made Marty think of graceful dancers with their arms outstretched.

Brenda pointed out the bird feeders that hung from several trees at the edge of the lawn. A colorful variety of birds flocked around them. "Hank built the feeders," she told Marty. "He fills them with cracked corn, sun-flower seeds, and some other stuff. It's his own secret blend."

Marty was surprised. "Really? I wouldn't have guessed he was a bird-lover."

Brenda grinned. "Hank looks tough, but on the inside, he's a real softie. Don't tell him I said so, though. It would ruin his image."

"There's nothing wrong with a little sensi-tivity. I like that in a guy," Marty objected.

"Like Darrin, I suppose?"

Marty frowned. "What's that supposed to mean?"

"It means that Darrin's got the sensitivity of an igneous rock, and you let him get away with it!" Brenda told her.

Marty shrugged and flashed a wry grin. It was hard to get mad at Brenda. "When you run into Mr. Perfect, let me know."

Brenda laughed. "Get real! If I do, he's all mine!"

The drone of an engine drowned out their laughter. A tractor-drawn gathering tank lumbered out of the woods, its chained wheels jingling as it chugged toward the girls.

"Here's Hank with a load of sap. Come on, let's watch him dump it." Brenda caught Marty's arm and tugged her toward the far end of the sugar house.

Hank steered the tank alongside an underground cistern next to the sugar house. Catching sight of them, he smiled and waved.

"Hard at work already?" Brenda called.

"Someone has to be. The sap ran all night and the gathering crew isn't coming until ten."

"I'd give you a hand, but I promised Gram I'd work in the salesroom," Brenda said.

"As if you'd be any help hauling sap," Hank teased. His smile widened to include Marty. He climbed off the tractor and fitted an extension to the movable pipe on the gathering tank. "Gathering sap's a little too much like real work for Brenda's taste."

Brenda kicked snow at her cousin. "Labeling syrup, stocking shelves, waiting on customers, guiding tours—that's not *real* work? Is that what you're saying, *Harold*?"

"Okay, okay! You're a regular working fiend!" Laughing, Hank spread the filter over the square, screened opening on top of the cistern, then lowered the pipe. Sparkling-clear sap gushed through the filtered opening into the cistern.

"Where does it go from here?" Marty asked.

Hank pointed to the sugaring house. "It's piped underground and fed automatically into the evaporating pans. Ever been in a sugaring house?"

Marty shook her head.

"Why don't you take her in and show her around?" Brenda suggested.

"I would, but I've got to get back out as soon as this unloads. I've got buckets running over."

"Maybe I can help. Just tell me what to do," Marty offered.

Hank's expression was doubtful as he looked her up and down. "It's pretty heavy work. The guys'll be along in a while."

Before Marty could retort that small didn't necessarily mean weak, Brenda said, "Give her a break, you maple-syrup chauvinist!"

Hank gave them both a good-natured grin, then lifted the pipe, changed the filter and lowered it again. He took the soiled filter down to the far end of the cistern and turned on the pump to rinse it out. Brenda quickly followed him.

Out of the corner of her eye, Marty saw Brenda jabbering away to Hank. She couldn't hear her words, but she knew by Hank's glance in her direction that Brenda was talking about her.

Brenda's voice grew louder. "Oh, come on! You could at least let her ride on the tractor. How much trouble can she be?"

Trouble! Is that what he thought about her? Marty's face burned. She never should have let Brenda talk her into coming out here! As she turned away, Marty noticed that the sap feeding into the cistern was about to overflow. She dashed forward and raised the extension pipe. Then Hank came up behind her and pushed the pipe all the way up.

"The holding tank must be full," Marty said.

"No, it's the flannel filter—the fibers clog. You have to keep changing it. Thanks for catching it," he added, the warmth of his voice beginning to melt her defenses.

Brenda beamed. "See? Didn't I tell you Marty's not helpless?"

Marty lifted her chin and grabbed Brenda's sleeve. "Come on, Bren. I'll help *you* in the shop."

24

"Good idea," Hank said. "Girls aren't cut out for timber work. It's wet and heavy and cold and . . ."

"Wait a second!" Marty cut in angrily. "Just for the record, I figure if you can do it, I can do it. Not that I want to," she added quickly. "But if I *did* want to, I could!"

Hank said solemnly. "All things being equal, I'm sure you could."

"Meaning?" Marty demanded.

He looked her up and down again. "It takes strength. And height doesn't hurt, either."

Even angrier now, Marty stood as tall as she could. "I'm not all *that* short!" she snapped.

"You're not all that tall, either," he said with a grin.

Brenda grabbed Marty's arm. "Take it easy, guys. I don't want to see a fight between my best friend and my favorite cousin."

But Marty just glared at Hank. "You tell me what to do, and we'll see who can handle what!"

His mouth twitched as he tried not to smile. "You're not exactly dressed for it."

"What do you mean I'm not dressed for it?" Marty yelled. "I've got on enough clothes to scale the North Pole without getting a goose bump!"

"Yeah, but you're going to get dirty."

Suddenly Marty realized that her mother had been right about the pale-blue ski outfit. But she squared her shoulders and between clenched teeth muttered, "They'll wash."

Hank shrugged. "All right, then. Grab a couple of gathering buckets and climb on the trailer. Unless you want to drive," he added.

Not about to give him the satisfaction of showing her up, Marty waved aside his offer. "You go ahead. You know your way through the woods."

Nodding, Hank raised the extension pipe, climbed onto the tractor seat, and glanced back. "Coming?"

Marty pulled her hat farther down over her ears and climbed up on the trailer as Hank put the tractor into gear and started down the incline.

"Have fun, you guys," Brenda called after them, grinning.

Fat chance, thought Marty grimly. But she pasted on a carefree grin and waved to Brenda. Just as she did, Hank pulled on the throttle and the rig lurched forward. Marty grabbed the lipped edge of the gathering tank just in time to prevent herself from falling off. The track they were following into the woods was so rutted that the tractor and trailer wobbled from side to side, flinging mud every which way.

Marty set her jaw and hung on. Her pale-blue outfit was not going to come out of this looking good. But mud or no mud, Hank Maxwell would soon see he was wrong about her. She'd prove she could do this job just as well as any boy!

Chapter Four

Marty was glad the bite of the breeze was less noticeable now that they were among the trees. She certainly didn't want to give Hank the satisfaction of seeing her shiver.

The sun filtered through the bare branches and glinted off the capped buckets hanging from the sugar maples. Hank's off-key whistling, the puttering of the tractor engine, and the jingling of the tire chains made pleasant music as they rode deeper into the woods.

But the ride wasn't a comfortable one. The gathering tank took up most of the trailer space, leaving only a few narrow inches on the sides of the platform where Marty clung. And Marty was sure that Hank was deliberately hitting every bump in the road.

Dodging occasional flying blobs of mud, Marty edged bit by bit to the back of the trailer where there was a little more room and less mud. Just as she got settled, Hank stopped the rig. He came back to the trailer and grabbed his gathering pails. Marty jumped to the ground and reached for her pails, too.

"What do I do?" she asked when he started away without a word.

Hank paused and pointed to a tree right next to the rig. "The ones with the buckets are maples."

"I kind of figured that," Marty said dryly.

Faint crinkles fanned out from Hank's brown eyes as he grinned. "That's a start. You empty the ones close to the road, I'll go deep." The snow crunched beneath his feet as he strode past her and resumed whistling.

Marty set her gathering pails on the ground, then, realizing she had no idea what to do next, she turned to watch Hank. He pulled a bucket off a tree and poured the contents into his gathering pail in one smooth motion. Rehanging the bucket, he moved on to the next and emptied it just as efficiently.

Marty leaned over and peered beneath the curved cap on the bucket before her. It hung from the hook of a tap, one end of which was driven into the tree. Maple sap dripped from

the open end of the tap into the already overflowing bucket and splashed down her ski
pants.

"This one's running over," she called.

"A few of them are. Try not to get wet. Once
you do, the cold air goes right through you,"
Hank called back cheerfully.

Marty gingerly slipped the bucket off the
hook. The gathering tank was so close that
she decided to dump the bucket there rather
than into her pails. Resting it on the ridge
of the tank, Marty upended the bucket and
watched the contents swirl down and disappear through the funneled opening.

"This stuff's just like water," she muttered.
She pulled off a glove and caught a drip from
the tap on her finger before rehanging the
bucket. "Tastes like water, too." She called to
Hank, "What do you add to make it thicken?"

"Nothing," he called back. "It's the process
of evaporation. We just keep boiling and boiling it, and the water evaporates, leaving the
syrup."

"And it turns maple-colored?"

"The sugar content makes it turn. De-
pending on the sweetness of the sap, it can
take up to fifty gallons of the stuff to make a
gallon of syrup," Hank told her.

Fifty gallons! From then on, Marty took a
little more care not to spill any. But despite

her efforts, the sap sloshed out and her gloves got wet as she handled the next two buckets. The dampness seeped through, chilling her fingers.

Each time they finished covering an area, Hank drove the tractor forward. Muscles aching, Marty was glad he left the trees close to the road for her. And by now her hands were freezing and she'd even spilled sap into her boots!

Hank must have sensed she was getting tired, because the next time they approached the gathering tank at the same time, he emptied his own pails, then reached for hers.

"I can do it," Marty insisted. She stood on her tiptoes to heave up the lighter of the two, her arms throbbing with exhaustion. As she upended the pail, part of the sap splashed into the tank, but the rest caught Hank full in the face.

He wiped the sleeve of his coat across his wet cheeks. "That's twice now. Am I wrong, or are you and anything liquid a dangerous combination?"

Remembering the incident in her kitchen, Marty couldn't help smiling. "Only when you're around."

"In that case . . ." He reached for her remaining gathering pail, and Marty let him take it. What little strength she had left in her arms was fading fast. She scooted out of Hank's way, saying, "I won't get it so full next time." After a moment, she added, "You were partially right, I guess, though it's height and muscle, not sex, that gives a person the edge."

"Willingness is worth a lot, too," he said.

There was a note of appreciation in his voice that made Marty have second thoughts. Had she been wrong about him? Her earlier irritation mellowing, she ventured, "Is it a draw, then?"

He looked at her with a twinkle in his eye. "A draw? I didn't know we were having a contest."

"Oh, so you didn't say this was work for guys?" she challenged.

"I said it was *heavy* work."

"And what about fixing a light plug?" Marty persisted. "Is that heavy work too?"

He looked bewildered for a moment, then apparently realized what she was referring to. "Hey, I was just lending a hand."

"Right. And I appreciated it. But today *I* offered to lend a hand, and what did you do?"

"Okay, okay. I apologize," Hank said with a sheepish grin. "Now would you stop being so stubborn and give me a chance?"

"A chance for what?" she asked suspiciously.

"A chance to prove I'm not the jerk you seem to think I am."

Marty smiled at him. Instead of answering, she sang a lyric from a song that was in her head: " 'It don't hafta burn to be stubborn; don't let 'em say it can't be done.' "

"Phantom Spry, right?" he asked, grinning.

Marty nodded. " 'Don't Let 'Em Say You Can't.' I love their stuff."

"So do I," Hank said. "Okay, it's a draw. Case closed?"

She nodded happily and they went back to work.

Suddenly Hank touched Marty's arm and whispered, "There's a deer. Look!"

She peered in the direction he was pointing, but didn't see it. "Where?"

Grabbing her hand, Hank pulled her along a few yards. "There! Behind the bush!"

Marty caught a flash of white tail, then a blur of movement as the deer bounded over a dead log and away. Heart pounding, she exclaimed, "It's beautiful! I've never seen a deer up close before."

"They're hard to spot because they blend in with the woods and snow." Hank's voice reflected his own pleasure in the deer. He let go of her hand and pushed a low branch out of their way.

"I'll bet you see them all the time," Marty said.

"Yeah, but it's always exciting. When the snow is real deep, Dad and I put hay out in the field for them. I sneak up and watch them eat—fifteen or twenty of them feeding at one time. 'Course, they catch wind of you, and they're gone. Their keen sense of smell and their speed is what makes them so challenging to hunt."

Marty caught her breath in dismay. "You *hunt* them?"

"I thought I would last fall. I got a license, did some scouting ahead of time, found myself a good lookout. Had a perfect shot at an eight-point buck. . . ." His voice trailed off.

"And?" Marty prompted.

Hank shrugged. "I kept telling myself our area's overpopulated with them, but I couldn't bring myself to pull the trigger. I got some good snapshots, though."

"Good for you," Marty said, relieved.

Looking a little embarrassed, Hank picked up his pails and resumed gathering, and Marty did the same. All her muscles were aching by the time Hank announced, "Tank's full—let's take her in. You want to drive?"

"I can drive a car, but I don't know anything about tractors," she admitted.

He gave her a cheerful grin. "Then here's your chance to learn. Come on, it's all yours."

"You're sure your grandfather won't mind?" Marty asked.

He chuckled. "Are you kidding? He'd put that crazy cat of yours in the seat if he thought he could drive."

Reassured, Marty hopped up onto the tractor seat, then looked over the controls blankly.

"There's not much to driving Old Smokey," Hank told her. "When you want to stop, just push in the clutch with your foot there. Use it to shift, too."

"And when I want to go?"

"Put her in gear. Push in the clutch first."

Marty followed his instructions and the engine roared. "What now?"

He climbed up beside her and perched on a toolbox that was attached to the left fender. Pointing out the shifting knob between her knees, he said, "Put her into second. Over and up, like the diagram on the knob—there you go. Now let the clutch out easy."

Marty lifted her foot. The tractor jumped forward and stalled.

"A little easier next time." Dropping down to the trailer hitch, Hank clung to the seat with one hand and braced his other hand on the tractor's left fender. Leaning forward so that his chin was just inches from Marty's shoulder, he pointed out another lever. "The throttle's on the right-hand side of the steering column. Pull it down."

Marty put her hand on the lever and did as she was told. The tractor lurched forward again, this time humming a higher note. She tightened her grip on the wheel as they sloshed through a puddle in the road.

"Relax," Hank said. "As long as you keep the wheels in the ruts, you can't go wrong."

"Unless I get stuck."

"If you do, you do." Hank grinned at her and added, "Kind of a bumpy ride, isn't it?"

Marty nodded, but for some reason it didn't seem as bumpy as it had on the way out. Despite her concentration on her driving, Marty was keenly aware of Hank's nearness. She liked the way his hair curled in wisps from under his cap, and the quick flash of dimples when he smiled. An image of Darrin flitted briefly through her mind, but she knew it wasn't the thought of Darrin that made her pulse pound so wildly.

Chapter Five

As Marty helped Hank empty the load of sap into the cistern, the gathering crew arrived—Hank's uncle, his two brothers-in-law, and Hank's friend, Orin.

Recognizing Marty, Orin shouted, "Hey, it's the water girl! Came out to help Brenda, did you?"

"Yes, she did," Hank answered for her. "But I stole her away. She's been helping me gather."

"So that's how you got wet!" Orin slapped Hank on the back and they both laughed.

The crew went out to the timber with a second gathering rig while Hank waited for the first one to empty.

"We shuttle the two rigs back and forth.

39

That way, we don't lose a lot of time," he explained to Marty. Noticing her wet gloves and damp ski pants, he added, "Why don't you go into the shop and warm up?"

Marty agreed that it would be a good idea. Thinking that Hank would call her before he headed back into the timber, she kicked off her boots at the door and went inside, wiggling her numb toes. Brenda paused in sweeping the shop to fix her a cup of hot cocoa. Marty was drinking the last of it when she glanced out the window and saw the gathering rig pull out.

"Hank's leaving without me!" she cried.

Brenda shrugged. "He's got a full crew now. Guess he doesn't need you anymore."

Marty frowned as the rig disappeared down a timber road. She turned away from the window, feeling oddly disappointed and left out.

"There's plenty for you to do right here," said Brenda briskly. "We've got half-a-dozen tour groups scheduled. I'll show you the ropes here in the shop. Then Gram and I will show the groups around while you sell."

After Marty slipped out of her soiled ski pants and jacket, Brenda's grandmother gave her a pair of dry sneakers. Then Marty learned how to operate the cash register while Brenda went out to meet a busload of senior citizens that had just pulled in. The rest of the morning passed in a blur of activity. Marty was so busy that lunch was just a sandwich on the run.

"Must be the last load—the guys are rinsing their boots," Brenda announced as the late afternoon sun slipped behind the trees.

"Guess we'd better call it a day, too." Brenda's grandmother turned the sign on the shop door around to "Closed."

Marty glanced at her watch. "Is it really that late? Darrin's supposed to be picking me up in half an hour. He wants to catch the early movie."

Brenda's grandmother paid Marty for her day's work and urged her to come back again the following Saturday. Marty accepted, happy at the prospect of earning more money. She bought the syrup she'd promised her mother and tossed her muddy boots into the trunk of Brenda's car. Hank and Orin approached, waving.

"Are you two coming back tomorrow?" Hank asked.

"I can't," said Marty. "We always spend Sunday afternoons at my grandmother's house."

"Ancient Evans tradition," Brenda said with a grin at Orin. "But I'll be here right after lunch."

Orin rubbed his stomach. "Speaking of food, I'm starved. Let's drive to Spring Junction and eat at Jedediah's. Ever been there? They fry up a slab of beef, tuck it between sourdough buns and pile on so much stuff you need three hands to hold onto it."

"Sounds good to me. How about you, Marty?" Brenda asked.

"Sorry—I'm running late already," Marty reminded her.

"That's right. Darrin," Brenda said, making a face.

"I'll drive Marty home," Hank offered. "There are a few things I need to pick up in town anyway."

"Great!" Beckoning to Orin, Brenda opened her car door. "Then we can take my car."

Marty glanced at her watch again as Hank led the way to a pickup truck that looked older than both of them. It was the same truck that had been parked in Brenda's drive the previous week. As Hank opened the passenger door for her, he said, "Grandpa's old truck isn't in the best of shape." He looked apologetic.

Marty climbed in and fastened her seat belt.

"She's a little bumpy too," he said as the truck jerked down the lane. His cheeks creased into dimples as he added, "Bronco Betty—that's what we call her, because she'll buck you all the way to town and back."

It seemed that in no time at all Hank was turning into Marty's driveway. Darrin's parents' car was already there, Marty noticed with a twinge of guilt, and Darrin was sitting in it.

"Thanks a lot for the ride," she said, trying to open the door. She shoved against it with her shoulder, but it refused to budge.

"It won't open from the inside." Hank climbed out, came around and opened the door for her. "See you next Saturday," he called as he backed the pickup out of the driveway.

"Okay!" Marty waved, then ran to meet Darrin as he got out of his car. "Hi! Sorry I'm late," she said breathlessly.

Darrin's blue eyes were chilly under his thatch of thick blond hair. "I thought we were on for five-thirty," he said.

"I was working out at Bren's grandparents' maple camp. We were so busy, I lost track of time." Putting her key into the front door lock, Marty gave him her warmest smile. "Make yourself comfortable—I'll hurry."

"Who's the guy?" Darrin asked, following her inside.

"Hank Maxwell," Marty told him. "He's

Brenda's cousin. He works out there too," she added, surprised to find that Darrin looked annoyed. "I rode out with Brenda, but she wasn't ready to leave yet, so Hank offered to bring me home."

"Nice of him," Darrin said.

Deciding to ignore his irritation, Marty left Darrin watching TV. She dashed upstairs, showered in record time, flew into her clothes, and hurried back to the living room.

"So how come Brenda couldn't bring you home?" Darrin picked up where they'd left off as he helped Marty into her coat.

"She decided to go for something to eat with Orin."

"Orin who?"

Marty led the way out the door. "I don't remember his last name."

"Where does she meet all these guys, anyway?" Darrin asked.

Marty shrugged. "Search me. I guess she met Orin out at the syrup camp. He's a friend of Hank's."

As they got into the car, Darrin frowned. "Hank Maxwell. The name's kind of familiar. . . ."

"Maybe you've met him," Marty said. She went on to tell Darrin how she and Hank had worked together that morning.

"So you and this Maxwell guy went out into the timber alone?" he asked when she had finished.

His tone annoyed Marty. "We were *working*," she emphasized. "I spent my last cent on Phantom Spry tickets for you and me, so I figured I could use the money, and . . ."

"Phantom Spry?" Darrin interrupted, adjusting the car heater. "I didn't know we were going."

"I was going to surprise you," Marty said lamely.

Darrin stopped at the next intersection, waiting for the light to change. "I wish you'd asked me first. I'm not all that crazy about Phantom Spry."

"Well, I am," said Marty, feeling prickly all of a sudden. "It'll be my treat."

The film was a spy thriller. Between her growling stomach and her whirling thoughts, Marty had trouble tuning in. Darrin, on the other hand, seemed thoroughly engrossed. Or at least she thought he was, until midway through the film, he reached for her hand and whispered in her ear, "You could work at your mom's furniture store, couldn't you? I mean, why go clear out to that maple camp when your mom would give you a job right here in town?"

"I guess so," she murmured, returning the pressure of his hand. "But it's kind of fun, learning something new."

"*Learning* something new, or *meeting* someone new?"

Marty felt uncomfortable at the accusing tone of Darrin's voice. Face heating up, she insisted, *"Learning."* In the semidarkness, she saw the muscle along his jawline working. He dropped her hand. "So what'd this guy teach you?"

Disliking his tone as much as his words, Marty's temper rose. "Maybe you better explain what you mean by that!"

"Really? I thought it was pretty clear."

"I don't believe this!" Marty exclaimed. "You're jealous!"

"I guess I've got a right to be," he hissed back at her. "We're supposed to be going steady and here I find out you've spent the whole day with another guy!"

"Shhh! We can't hear!" a couple of kids protested behind them.

Darrin lapsed into a sulky silence. It was all downhill after that. By the time their date was over, they were barely speaking. Darrin pulled into Marty's driveway and left the engine running as he walked her to the door.

D.C. had gotten shut out of the garage. He

was waiting beneath the porch light, and Marty bent down to pick him up. In a stilted voice, she said goodnight. Darrin gave her a curt nod and strode back down the walk without another word.

Chapter Six

On Sunday, Marty went with her parents to her grandmother Evans's house. Her uncle Simon and his wife and children came too. After a late lunch, Marty's niece and nephew grew so noisy that Marty's mother suggested that she take them down to the park.

It seemed a good idea at the time, but the wind was cold, and the children were soon tired of playing on the swings. Anna demanded to be picked up, and Brett whined that his hands were cold. Marty was carrying Anna in one arm and clinging to Brett's mittened hand when she saw a car that looked like Darrin's coming down the street.

"I think that's Darrin," Marty said to the

kids. "He's slowing down! Quick, let's catch a ride!"

But the car picked up speed again and drove off before she could catch up to it. "Maybe it wasn't Darrin after all," she told the disappointed children. Still, she couldn't help feeling that Darrin had deliberately avoided her.

Marty didn't see Darrin again until Monday at school. She and Brenda shared the last class of the morning, and as they came down the corridor together, they found Darrin waiting near Marty's locker. As a rule, he rushed down to the cafeteria and saved her a place at "their" corner table. Caught off-guard, Marty pushed a blond tendril back from her forehead and asked brightly, "Going my way?"

Somber-faced, Darrin shifted from foot to foot. "We need to talk."

"Now?"

"I don't think so. Alone would be better." He gave Brenda a pointed look.

Brenda smirked at him. "So how's it going, Darrin? Taken out any mailboxes lately?"

Marty winced at Brenda's words. Darrin had sideswiped a mailbox nearly two weeks ago while he was driving a friend home. He'd broken the right headlight on his red vintage Mustang and done a fair amount of damage to the bumper and grille. The car was still in the body shop. "That mailbox was too close to the road," Darrin grumbled.

"Well, maybe if they'd had the flag up . . ." Brenda shot Darrin a taunting grin and gave Marty a little wave as she headed for the cafeteria.

Though Marty had spent most of Sunday preparing herself for this talk, her heart squeezed painfully tight. She slipped into her coat and followed Darrin out the nearest exit.

Darrin leaned against the brick wall of the building and gazed over the top of Marty's head. "I remember who this Maxwell guy is. He's Woodland Grove's main man in track. He's a real good runner. He went to State last year and placed in two events. There was a big article about him on the sports page."

Puzzled, Marty said, "So?"

"So if you're going to chase after him, I thought I'd warn you he's pretty fast!"

The blood rushed to Marty's face. She stretched to her full height and retorted, "I'm *not* chasing after Hank Maxwell!"

Darrin shrugged. "That's what it looks like to me."

"How would you know? You weren't even there!" Marty was getting really angry.

"No, but you seemed pretty eager to go back. It's got to be more than the money. You said yourself that if you wanted to, you could work at the store for your mother."

"I *like* working for someone besides my parents!" Marty snapped. "Besides, I told Mrs. Kelly I'd come. She's counting on me." Realizing that it sounded as if she were making excuses, Marty continued, "Not that I have to explain to you. Where I work and who I work with is my own business!"

Darrin set his jaw in a firm line. "Okay, then. I guess I know where I stand. If you're going to keep seeing this guy, well then, maybe I'll start looking around too."

Trying to conceal her shock and surprise, Marty tipped her chin and said, "Suit yourself."

"You wouldn't be jealous?" Darrin asked.

"There's already too much of that going around," Marty snapped. Fighting stinging tears, she turned on her heel and scurried back into the building.

The girls' locker room was empty. Glad for the privacy, Marty dried her eyes. Darrin's jealousy made it clear that he didn't trust her. It was insulting not to be trusted! Without trust, what kind of future did they have together, anyway? Alone with her hurt and anger, Marty waited miserably for the bell to ring. Some Monday this was turning out to be!

*   *   *

The rest of the week wasn't any better. Mr. Coltry caught D.C. with the remains of a dead bird and threatened to call the town's Animal Control Division, and Marty's father had a major allergy attack—two strikes against D.C. Darrin didn't call once, and when Marty ran into him in the hall he always turned away and pretended not to see her.

On Friday Marty decided that it was up to her to smooth things over. She stopped Darrin in the hallway and asked how the repairs on his car were coming along.

"I'm picking it up from the body shop this afternoon," he said. Then, apparently uninterested in a reconciliation, he brushed past her. As he did, the wire of one of Marty's spiral notebooks caught in Darrin's cable-knit sweater, jerking the notebook and the books on top of it out of her hands. Books and papers scattered everywhere. Darrin scowled and paused to examine the damage to his sweater, but he didn't apologize, and he didn't help her gather up her books. Instead, he kept on walking and struck up a conversation with the pretty new foreign exchange student.

Face burning, Marty bent down to pick up her scattered things. How could Darrin be so rude? So just plain mean?

"Great new method of filing—throw it all on the floor!" Brenda joked as she dropped to her knees to help. She noticed Marty's stricken expression and looked around. Spotting Darrin and the beautiful exchange student, she whispered, "Chill out, Mart. He's just trying to make you jealous."

Brenda's loyalty made Marty feel a little better. She whispered back, "I'd like to tell him what I think of the way he's acting!"

"Don't give him the satisfaction. Pretend you couldn't care less."

Brenda handed Marty her books, and the two girls started down the hall. As they swept past Darrin, Brenda announced loudly, "Hank called last night. He was glad to hear you're going to help out again tomorrow, and he said to tell you to wear that same sexy ski outfit."

Marty stared at her friend in astonishment. "I can't *believe* he said that!" she exclaimed as Brenda dragged her along.

Brenda snickered. "Of course he didn't. I made it up. Two can play that game, you know," she added, aiming a pointed glance over her shoulder in Darrin's direction.

Marty looked back too, and caught Darrin staring after them, looking as miserable as she felt. So Brenda was right! He *was* playing games! Did that mean he still cared?

More importantly, after the way he'd behaved, did she *want* him to still care? Confused and uncertain, Marty let Brenda lead her outside.

As they walked to Brenda's car, Marty asked, "What did Hank *really* say?"

"He said the sap is going to be running and we can use all the help we can get."

"Any old hired hand will do, huh?" Marty said dryly.

Brenda shot her a curious look. "Forgive my confusion, but who are you moping over—Darrin or Hank?"

"Neither," Marty said firmly. She got into the car and fastened her seatbelt. "I'm done with moping. They can both take a hike for all I care!"

"Sure they can," Brenda said with a knowing grin.

As soon as Marty and Brenda arrived at the syrup camp on Saturday morning, Mrs. Kelly put them to work in the shop. For a while, business was brisk. But right after lunch it began to snow, and the flow of customers slowed to a trickle, then stopped altogether. By midafternoon, the weather bureau issued a travel advisory, and Mrs. Kelly closed the shop and urged the girls to stay until the snow let up.

"Gram, that could be sometime tomorrow," Brenda pointed out.

"True," said Mrs. Kelly. "Then why don't you both plan on spending the night?"

Both girls agreed, and Marty called her parents for their permission. An hour later, Hank and Orin tramped into the shop to warm up. Mrs. Kelly talked them out of starting home, too, at least until the snow let up.

After dinner, Hank and Brenda's grandparents retired to the living room while the boys helped Brenda and Marty with the dishes.

"Woman's work," complained Hank, rolling up his shirt sleeves.

"So what's man's work?" Marty retorted.

"Seeing that woman does *her* work!" Hank grinned and dodged the playful punch she aimed at him.

While the others were drying and putting dishes away, Hank disappeared into the next room and returned with a jigsaw puzzle.

Brenda took one look at the picture and groaned. "It's a jar of jellybeans! Look at all those tiny pieces! What are you trying to do, ruin my eyes?"

Grinning, Hank dumped the puzzle pieces on the kitchen table. "We'll save the edge pieces for you, crybaby. How about it, Marty? Are you any good at puzzles?"

"I'm not too bad," Marty said modestly.

Slipping into the nearest chair, she sifted through the pile and immediately fitted together the first two pieces.

"Beginner's luck," Hank grumbled, taking the chair next to hers.

Marty grinned. "Hold your applause until you've seen the instant replay."

"Only if you've got it in slow-mo," Hank joked.

Marty broke the two pieces apart and very, very slowly fitted them back together again.

Hank stared at her with mock awe. Turning to Brenda and Orin, he asked, "Did you ever see such skill? Such technique? Such unmatched, unparalleled, undisputed dexterity?"

Laughing, Marty stood up and took a bow. She had never had such silly fun in her whole life, certainly never with Darrin. He would probably think being snowed in way out in the country was the most boring thing in the world. *No doubt about it,* Marty thought as she sat back down, *Darrin and Hank couldn't possibly be more different.*

Chapter Seven

"Hey, I see where that one goes!" Brenda whisked a puzzle piece away from Hank. Taking it with her, she went over to the counter and tuned the radio to a popular rock station. Turning up the volume, she announced, "My fingers work faster to music."

"Your fingers aren't going to work at all if you don't leave my pieces alone," Hank teased. He reached out to retrieve the piece she'd taken and fitted it into place.

"Sure, hog all the easy ones." Brenda made a face at him. In a stage whisper, she warned Marty and Orin, "Watch out—when the puzzle's almost done, *Harold* always hides one or two so he can say he put in the last piece!"

"*You're* the one who does that!" Hank countered.

"So who are you going to believe—him or me?" Brenda demanded.

Brenda helped work the puzzle only a short while longer before losing all interest. Jumping to her feet, she said, "There's a Nintendo game in the family room. How about it, Orin?"

Orin was out of his chair in an instant. "You're on!"

"What about you two?" Brenda asked Marty and Hank.

"I think I'll stay with this," said Hank.

"Me too," Marty agreed.

Brenda and Orin left and took the radio with them. After all the hilarity and loud music, it was suddenly very quiet in the warm, cozy kitchen. Hank and Marty worked in easy companionship, steadily filling in pieces until only a small section remained unfinished.

"You're really good at this," Marty remarked, leaning back in her chair to admire their handiwork.

Hank's dimples deepened as he smiled. "I think we're both pretty terrific."

Marty's fingers brushed his as they reached for one of the few remaining puzzle pieces. It was odd—suddenly she felt shy after having been so at ease. Her pulse pounded in her throat and she caught Hank watching her. As they exchanged glances, Marty's heartbeat quickened.

The sizzle and pop of a low-burning ember sounded loud in the silence. Hank stretched his long legs, inadvertently bumping into her feet. "Sorry. Everybody complains about my big feet."

Marty laughed. "You too? My dad's always giving me a hard time about the size of *my* feet."

"My dad doesn't tease me," Hank said. "Lila's the one who gives me grief."

Marty drew back her own feet, the name "Lila" echoing in her head. Who was Lila?

"Lila?" she asked. But Hank didn't reply. He scraped back his chair and got up from the table. Marty watched him stir the hot coals before tossing another log on the fire. Then he crossed to the window and pulled the curtain aside, looking out at the falling snow.

Marty turned her gaze back to the puzzle, uncomfortable with the strange tension that had suddenly sprung up between them. To her relief, Brenda bounced into the room just then.

"Hey, Orin! Come look at this! They're nearly done!" Brenda winked at Marty as she deftly scooped up one of the few remaining pieces.

Hank spun away from the window and gave Brenda a sharp glance. "Watch her—she'll be up to her old tricks," he warned, his familiar grin back in place.

"Would you listen to him? He's so *suspicious!*" With a wicked smile, Brenda stealthily dropped the stolen piece into Marty's lap and sat down at the table. Orin joined them. For a few minutes, there was a frenzied tangle of hands as they all tried to fit the last pieces in. When only one space was left and no piece, Hank looked accusingly at Brenda and thrust out his open palm.

"Okay, hand it over."

"Hand *what* over? *I* don't have it, do I, Marty?" Brenda rolled innocent eyes in Marty's direction.

"I'm sure she doesn't," said Marty truthfully. Casually she lowered one hand to her lap to conceal the piece Brenda had dropped there.

Hank let out a long-suffering sigh. "Guess we'll have to do this the hard way. Orin, grab her feet! We'll turn her upside down and shake it out of her!"

Brenda jumped up and backed away, squealing, "I don't have it, I swear!"

"Then you shouldn't mind our checking."

As the boys started after Brenda, Marty slipped the last piece into place.

Backed into a corner, Brenda pointed to the now-complete puzzle and cried, "Look! What did I tell you?"

Hank swung around. His glance skipped from the puzzle to Marty and he grinned. "Partners in crime! I should have guessed! You know what I think, Orin? I think these two deserve to be dumped into the nearest snowdrift!"

"Sore loser!" Brenda accused, laughing.

"Good idea," Orin said. "It's not coming down nearly so hard—let's go out."

Brenda shook her head. "No way! I don't want my face washed in the snow!"

"You really think we'd do that?" Orin said in an injured tone.

"I don't think, I *know*!" Brenda shot back.

Grinning, Hank said, "Bren, you find the sled and promise me first turn down the hill, and I'll let bygones be bygones, okay?"

"Fair enough," Brenda agreed.

They all bundled up quickly and charged out into the snowy night. The dark sky was starless. Though the snow had nearly stopped, the wind skipped across the drifts, pelting Marty's cheeks with icy crystals. She sat down on the porch steps and pulled on her boots while Brenda headed for her grandfather's barn. The boys, armed with a flashlight, went with her. They all returned together, Hank pulling a long, heavy-duty sled.

"Grandpa made it years ago. It's indestructible!" Brenda said, puffing a little as they started off into the woods.

An owl hooted in the wintery night. Shivering at the eerie sound, Marty quickened her step. She'd always considered herself to be as brave as the next person, but she had lived all her life in town. The timber at night was another world.

Seeming to guess her nervousness, Hank flicked on the flashlight. "Snow's pretty deep. Makes things look different, doesn't it?"

Grateful for his understanding, Marty nodded. The beam of light was comforting, and she felt sure that Hank knew every tree in the forest.

They soon reached their destination, a steep, seldom-traveled back road blanketed in snow. Hank turned off the flashlight. Without the canopy of trees overhead, the snow-drifted road was clearly visible.

"You go first, that was the deal," Brenda said to Hank.

He positioned the sled in the middle of the road at the crest of the steep hill and belly flopped down on it. But before the others could give him a push, he stood up.

"I've decided to be a sport about this. Marty, you want to go first? Nothing to do with gender, of course," he added quickly, making her laugh.

"If it's all the same to you, I'd rather watch someone else before I try it," she said. "I don't know this hill at all. I'd probably end up wrapped around a tree."

"All right then, we'll both go." Hank sat down on the sled and scooted forward, making room for Marty, and she piled on behind him.

"Ready?" he called.

"Ready as I'll ever be!" Marty called back.

Orin gave them a push. There was ice beneath the snow, and once they were under way, the sled picked up speed. The dark trunks of trees on either side of the road flew past in a blur. The wind stung Marty's cheeks, burned her eyes, and made her nose tingle. She laughed in exhilaration as they hit a bump and nearly fell off.

"Hang on!" Hank yelled, and she lurched forward, wrapping her arms around him. Face buried in his back, she felt the rough weave of his coat against her cheek and the muscular strength of him in her arms. At the bottom of the hill, Hank skidded the sled sideways and they both tumbled off into a drift.

"You did that on purpose!" Marty cried, laughing. She rolled to her feet and pelted him with a handful of snow.

"Falling off is half the fun," Hank said and tackled her at the ankles as she stooped to form a snowball. With a shriek, Marty turned her face away from his gloved hands full of snow.

At the last moment, Hank flopped down beside her, tossed the snow up in the air and let it drift back down on both of them. Their mingled laughter echoed in the blustery air. Marty rolled over on her back, gazing up at the dark sky. Her cheeks were smarting from the cold and her toes were tingling. But deep inside, her heart was hot and throbbing in her chest.

"I love winter!" Hank said softly. "Everything's so beautiful. Listen to how quiet it is."

They both lay still, listening. They could hear Brenda and Orin calling from the top of the hill, but their voices were faint and far away.

"They're probably wondering where we are," Hank said.

Marty smiled in agreement. Her pulse quickened as Hank pulled one hand free of his glove and lightly brushed snowflakes from her face. His fingers felt warm on her cold skin, sending sparks all through Marty. And then, somewhere between laughter and a clear, sharp breath of night air, his lips touched hers in a cold, snowy kiss.

Chapter Eight

Before Marty could catch her breath, Hank was on his feet, pulling her out of the drift and mumbling an apology. Marty wanted to tell him there was nothing to be sorry about, but she was too stunned to speak. Frowning, Hank grabbed the sled rope and started up the hill with long-legged strides.

Marty lagged behind, her head spinning. It would be easy, in this dreamy white night, to think she'd only imagined his kiss. But the memory of it lingered shadowlike on her lips. She knew now that she had wanted him to kiss her, and obviously he had wanted it, too. What had happened? Why the swift change in him? The kiss had seemed so right. Marty was so confused that she stumbled in the snow.

Hank glanced back at her and hesitated as if there was something he needed to say.

"Cold?" he asked.

"A little," she panted.

"We can start back if you want to."

"I'll wait until Brenda and Orin are ready," Marty said, wiggling her icy toes in her boots.

"You're a good sport," he murmured in the darkness.

About the kiss? she wondered. *Or the cold?*

But Marty kept her questions to herself, and little by little, they regained some of their earlier ease with one another. But when it was their turn to go down the hill again, she was very careful to hold onto the sled, not Hank. This time he didn't spill them off, tackle her in the drifts, or sprinkle snowflakes on her face. And he didn't kiss her again, either.

Later that night, long after the boys had gone home, Marty snuggled beneath an old-fashioned quilt and whispered to Brenda, "Who's Lila?"

The springs squeaked as Brenda turned over in the bunk above her. "She's a girl Hank's been dating. . . . Why?"

Marty's heart sank. He already had a girlfriend!

"Are they serious?" she asked.

"I don't know about *serious*. But they've been going out for several months now. Personally, I've never been able to figure out what he sees in her."

But if Hank was dating Lila, why had he kissed her? Marty wondered. Confused, she tried to sort out her feelings. Her heart skipped at the memory of Hank's lips touching hers. She was deeply attracted to him, and for one brief moment, at the bottom of that snowy hill, she'd dared to hope he felt the same way. But when the kiss was over, he'd behaved so strangely, almost as if he couldn't get away from her fast enough. Had he been thinking about Lila? Did he feel guilty? What kind of guy was Hank Maxwell, anyway, kissing her while he was going out with someone else?

"Lila hardly ever comes out here," Brenda went on. "Afraid she'll get a little mud on her fancy shoes, I guess."

"Is she pretty?" Marty asked.

"Oh, she's okay, I guess. Kind of tall and slender with long, ash-blond hair."

Marty groaned and covered her ears with her pillow. *Forget it, he's taken!* she told herself. But when she closed her eyes, all she could think about was Hank kissing her in the snow. In another split second, she would have been kissing him back. What would have happened then?

Over the next several days, every time Marty thought about Hank, she tried to push him right out of her mind.

On Thursday, Marty's inner conflict came to a temporary halt when her father received the bill from the hospital for emergency room services after his last allergy attack. He was in the midst of a lecture on how Marty was going to have to keep D.C. locked in the garage so the house would be free of cat hair when her pet scratched on the screen. Marty opened the door leading out to the garage to find a dead cardinal on the doorstep.

"That does it!" Mr. Evans exclaimed. "When Coltry finds out about this, he'll raise the roof. That cat has to go!"

Marty slipped out into the garage and picked up D.C., stroking his velvet-smooth fur. He purred, arched his neck, and rubbed his head against her chin, the picture of loving innocence.

"You don't mean to be naughty, do you?" she whispered. "I guess you can't help going after birds—it's just your nature. When Dad calms down, he'll change his mind, you'll see."

But this time D.C. had gone too far.

"You've got one week to find him another home," Marty's father told her, and not even her mother could change his mind.

The next day at school, Marty was so worried about D.C. that she didn't notice Darrin standing by her locker until he said hello. After two weeks of being ignored, Marty was surprised.

"Something wrong?" she asked, nervously twirling her combination lock.

Darrin smiled at her. "I thought maybe we could do something tonight."

"But it's Friday. You always hang out with your friends on Friday nights."

"We're friends, aren't we?" he said quietly. "At least, we used to be." The earnest expression in his blue eyes softened Marty's heart. "I've been behaving like a jerk. I'm sorry, Marty," he added. "So how about it? Will you go out with me?"

Marty looked at him for a long moment. There were a lot of good things about Darrin, things she'd found very appealing over the past few months. But somehow, the emotional tug was no longer there. The memory of a sled ride down a snowy hill flitted through Marty's mind. Averting her gaze, she said, "As a friend, Darrin. I'll go as a friend. Okay?"

"Okay," he agreed. Smiling again, he added, "I'll pick you up about seven."

Marty's father surprised her that evening with a gift of a deep-brown oilskin "outback" coat. All winter she'd been admiring it in the window of Wild Country, the clothing store next to her mother's furniture store. A "range coat," her father called it. It had a loose fit, a cape-like yoke, and a slit up the back like the long slickers cowboys wore as they galloped across rain-swept praries in old western movies. Though she realized that it was supposed to soften the blow of his ultimatum concerning D.C., Marty was still delighted.

She put it on, then ran to her room for the old felt fedora she'd bought several months earlier at a vintage clothing store. Flipping her hair out from under the hat, Marty dashed back downstairs and pirouetted in front of her parents.

"Is this hot, or what?"

"Good grief!" her mother exclaimed. "It's Calamity Jane!"

Her father laughed. "I think she looks terrific!"

Marty hugged him. "Thanks, Dad. I love it!"

"I'm sorry about the cat," he said gently. "If my allergies were the only problem, I'd look into taking shots. But this business with Mr. Coltry . . ." His voice trailed off, and he sighed. "Find him a good home. But hurry, honey, before this bird business turns into an all-out feud."

Darrin arrived right on time. He gave her new coat an odd look, and once they were in his car, he complained that it smelled funny.

"That's the oil. It's what keeps it waterproof," Marty explained. "I bet I could gather sap in this thing and not get a bit wet."

Darrin concentrated on his driving. "So you're still going out there?"

"It's an interesting place to work. I enjoy it," Marty said defensively.

"What about this Maxwell guy? You still seeing him?" Darrin asked.

Marty stared straight ahead. "I never was *seeing* him, not in the way you mean," she said quietly. "We just work together. Besides, he's got a girlfriend."

By the dashboard's dim light, she saw Darrin raise one eyebrow. "Tough break," he said.

Marty felt her face flushing. "What's that supposed to mean?"

"Nothing. Just . . . tough break."

Marty sighed. He'd known how she felt

about Hank from the very beginning, even before she'd known for sure herself. They drove in silence for a while. At last Marty asked in a small voice, "How'd you guess?"

"About that guy Maxwell?" Darrin shrugged. "I don't know. I guess maybe it was the way you looked at him when you climbed out of that old beat-up truck the first time you went out to the syrup camp. You used to look at me like that."

Marty glanced over at him, sudden tears of remorse in her eyes. She said softly, "I'm sorry."

Darrin smiled a little. "You can't help what you feel. Yeah, I was mad for a while—it kind of hurt my pride, you know? But the more I thought about it, the more I realized I'd been having some of those feelings, too. Only I wouldn't admit it to myself."

"About who?" Marty asked before she could stop herself. When Darrin didn't answer, she persisted, "Someone I know? It *is*! It's someone I know, isn't it?"

"Maybe. Jealous?" he asked, glancing over at her.

There was a twinge, Marty couldn't deny it. "A little, I guess. But I'm not mad," she added quickly.

"Good. I was hoping you'd feel that way, because you might be able to help me," Darrin said as he turned in at the Golden Horn, a burger place where a lot of local kids hung out.

"How?" Marty asked, puzzled.

"Oh, maybe by putting in a good word for me."

Marty trotted after him as he climbed out of the warm car and dashed across the cold parking lot. "You've got to tell me who!"

"I will—later."

Marty had to be satisfied with that. Over bacon cheeseburgers, fries, and sodas, she told Darrin about having to find a new home for D.C. He offered a sympathetic comment or two, but Marty had the feeling he wasn't really listening. He kept gazing past her at someone she couldn't see, and he didn't look happy.

When she turned around, Marty saw Brenda and Orin in a back booth, holding hands. Marty stared from Darrin's glum face to the couple in the booth and back to Darrin again. It took a couple of minutes for her to get the picture.

"Brenda?" she squawked. "My best friend?"

Darrin's face turned brick red. That was all the confirmation Marty needed.

"But you two fight like cats and dogs!"

"Yeah—well, it's all a front, for me at least." He lifted his shoulders in a helpless shrug.

"I know it's crazy. I'm not her type. But lately I keep thinking about her, wishing she'd . . . you know, give me a chance."

Marty turned her head to stare at Brenda again, still struggling with the shock of Darrin's news. Brenda was his exact opposite—whimsical, disorganized, free-spirited, saying whatever popped into her head. Marty couldn't think of a more unlikely couple at Riverton High.

"Will you help me, Marty?" Darrin asked earnestly.

Marty's thoughts raced on. Darrin was a serious kind of guy. Brenda, on the other hand, was never serious about anyone. It would never work! Marty started to protest, then changed her mind. Darrin wasn't asking for her opinion, he was asking for her help. She sipped the last of her drink and said weakly, "I'll see what I can do. But in return, you've got to do something for me."

"Shoot," Darrin said.

"Start asking around. I've got to find a good home for D.C."

He grinned. "It's a deal. And thanks, Marty. You're a good sport."

"People keep telling me that," she murmured, thinking of Hank. Now that she and Darrin were no longer a couple, Marty was free to admit to herself that Hank was the one she really cared about. But it wouldn't do her any good. Hank had a steady girl-friend, and kiss or no kiss, Marty was the one left out in the cold.

Chapter Nine

"Bren? Aren't you coming?" Marty asked the following morning.

"I've got a horrible sore throat," Brenda croaked. "I meant to call you, but I guess I overslept."

"Then we're not working today?"

"I told Gram I thought I'd better just stay in bed."

"Oh."

"But that's no reason for you to stay home," Brenda continued. "In fact, I kind of promised Gram you'd be out this afternoon. She's going to be shorthanded if you don't go. Oh, and Marty? If Orin asks about me, tell him I'm sick, and tell him I said not to stop by tonight or tomorrow night, either."

Familiar with this pattern of Brenda's, Marty asked suspiciously, "So are you *really* sick? Or just avoiding Orin?"

"A little of both," Brenda admitted with a raspy chuckle.

"You looked like you were having a good time at the Golden Horn last night," Marty said. "What happened?"

"Nothing, exactly. Except Orin started acting possessive, and I'm just not into that."

"What do you mean?"

"Well, you know when you and Darrin stopped by our table and I told Darrin I'd heard a rumor he was number one on the Ten Most Wanted list at the post office?"

"And he told you to Express Mail yourself to the dead-letter office?" Marty giggled.

Brenda's laughter gave way to a fit of coughing. When she had caught her breath again, she went on, "Anyway, after you left, Orin started acting all jealous. Over *Darrin*! As if he were *competition*, or something! I mean, *really*!"

Remembering her deal with Darrin, Marty said casually, "Not to take Orin's side, but I wouldn't rule it out entirely. After all, he *is* back in circulation."

Brenda sneezed, then asked, "Who?"

"Darrin." The silence that followed made Marty have second thoughts about Brenda's true feelings for Darrin. "Bren? You still there?"

"You and Darrin broke up, then?" Brenda sounded amazed. "But when I saw you together last night . . ."

"We decided to go back to being just friends," Marty told her.

"Well, what do you know! And after he was so mean to you, too!" Brenda sneezed again.

"Bless you!" Marty laughed. "He apologized for that. Darrin's really a pretty nice guy, Bren. I guess we just kind of outgrew each other, that's all." Then, as if the idea had suddenly occurred to her, "You know what? I bet he'd ask you out if you gave him a little encouragement."

Brenda surprised her a second time by asking, "You wouldn't mind?"

Marty hesitated. "No, Bren, I don't mind at all," she said, and realized that she meant it.

"Maybe I'll think about it," Brenda murmured.

Marty borrowed her father's car and drove out to the syrup camp through a cold rain that washed away last week's snow. Between waiting on customers, Marty helped Brenda's grandmother label syrup and stock the shelves in the shop.

Late in the afternoon, Mrs. Kelly returned from a quick trip to the cooking room. "Must be a virus going around," she said. "Orin went home early, and now Mr. Kelly's coming down with it. I made him go to bed. Hank's running the evaporator. Why don't you see if he could use some help, Marty?"

Marty left the shop and went into the main part of the building. The fragrant steam billowing around the large room made for limited vision. Marty stood getting her bearings a moment before she spotted Hank at the other end of the evaporator. It was the first time she had seen him since the night of the big snowstorm.

To Marty's dismay, her heartbeat quickened and her palms grew damp. All week, she had kept telling herself she hadn't known Hank long enough or well enough to have fallen for him so hard. They would be friends, nothing more. But as she watched him stir the sap with a big square ladle, she knew she'd only been fooling herself. She hadn't forgotten Hank's kiss—perhaps she never would. Why had he kissed her in the first place? And why couldn't she erase it from her mind? He obviously wasn't the guy for her, since he'd kissed her while he was going with Lila. Her cheeks flushed as Hank turned and saw her.

He smiled. "Hi! Gram said she was sending reinforcements."

"I'm not sure I know enough to be much help," said Marty, coming over to him through the wafting steam.

"The whole operation is pretty simple, once you understand it," he said, pointing out the pipes that fed sap from the outdoor cistern into the evaporator. He explained how the sap moved through the long sectioned pans, boiling away excess moisture until, through the process of evaporation, it reached what he called "near-syrup." At that point, it was drawn off by bucket, then poured into a round vat in the finishing room.

"After it's cooked to syrup, it's filtered again, then bottled hot," Hank said, bringing the brief tour to an end in the finishing room.

"So what do you want me to do?" Marty asked.

"How about bottling for me?"

Marty nodded and Hank brought over some cases of empty bottles and showed her how the bottling was done. Resting his hand on the spigot of the bottling tank, he warned, "You have to watch real close, or you'll run the bottles over. If that happens, rinse them off over at the sink. If you have any questions or need help, just yell," he added.

Marty went to work filling bottles with the sweet amber syrup and tightening the caps. In the next room Hank continued to run the evaporator, leaving the door between the two rooms open. Though the evaporator and the boiling sap made so much noise that talking was difficult, Marty and Hank shouted occasional comments back and forth. It was definitely not the time or place for a personal conversation.

Hank finally shut down the evaporator and carried the cases of syrup Marty had bottled into the storeroom. "Hungry?" he asked when the last box was put away.

"Half-starved," Marty admitted.

"Let's go see if Gram's got something to eat. Unless you want to go home, that is."

"Are we finished working?" Marty asked.

"There's still fifteen gallons in the finishing pan to be cooked after supper, and there's more bottling and some cleanup. But you can call it a day if you want to," he told her.

On impulse, Marty said, "If you're staying, I'll stay too."

Hank grabbed his dark-green poncho from a hook by the door. "Better get your coat— it's raining again."

Marty got her coat from the shop, slipped it on and grabbed her fedora. Hank was waiting for her by the door. He whistled as she came toward him. "That's some coat! You look like a desperado!"

Marty put on her hat, explaining, "Dad said I have to find my cat a new home. He gave me this coat as a kind of peace offering."

"A bribe, huh?" Hank grinned down at her. He reached out and tugged at the brim of her hat.

Marty tipped her head back. Hank's nearness was so distracting that for a moment she forgot her concern over D.C. His brown eyes were so warm and friendly. Was friendship all he wanted from her?

"I'm sorry," Hank murmured, a husky note in his voice. "You're upset about your cat, aren't you?" Opening the door for her, he draped an arm across her shoulder. "It may not make you feel any better, but there's a chance I can help you find a home for him."

Marty blinked in surprise. "You can? Really?"

Hank nodded. "He's a black cat, isn't he? What's his name again? B.C.?"

"D.C.," Marty corrected. "As in Washington."

"Well, if you're sure your father's not going to change his mind, I happen to know someone who's looking for a black cat."

"Is it someone who'll give him a good home?"

"You bet. Gourmet cat food, a rhinestone collar, and a lawn as big as a football field. That ought to make D.C. happy, don't you think?"

Before she could reply, Hank opened the door. It was raining in sheets. Lightning streaked the dark sky. Hank caught her hand and dragged her out into the downpour, shouting over a loud peal of thunder, "Race you to the house, Desperado!"

Mrs. Kelly served them hot soup, cornbread, and fresh apple cobbler. They lingered over it, enjoying every bite. Then Marty called home to let her parents know that she had had supper and would be working a while longer.

By the time Marty and Hank returned to the sugar house, the rain had stopped, the clouds had blown away, and the stars were beginning to shine. The night smelled fresh and clean. Marty returned to bottling syrup while Hank started the flame beneath the vat of near-syrup.

"How do you know when it's ready?" Marty asked.

"The thermometer here. Gotta keep a close eye on it," he said, giving the thermometer a tap.

As Marty leaned closer, trying to read the

thermometer, she heard Hank yell, "Watch out!"

His warning came a second too late. The open flame licked at Marty's shirttail. With a cry of alarm, she jumped back. Hank grabbed a basin of water and slung it at her. Then he dashed to the sink, refilled it and doused her shirt again. As he went back a third time, Marty yelped, "That's enough! It's out—don't drown me!"

"Are you hurt?" Hank asked anxiously.

"No, I'm fine," Marty assured him, though she was a little shaken.

"No burns?"

"None at all."

"You're sure?" Hank asked, his voice full of concern.

"Really! I'm fine!"

It had all happened so fast, it took them both a moment to recover. Wringing the water from her blackened shirttails, Marty cocked her head to one side and looked up at Hank. She began to see some humor in the situation. "Boy! When you get even, you *really* get even!"

He looked at her blankly, and she added with mock severity, "One tiny glass of water and a few drops of sap, that's all the damage I did. But *you!* Well, just look at me!"

Hank *did* look. It was such a long, leisurely look that Marty's face began to burn. He started to grin. The grin turned into a chuckle, and finally into laughter.

Marty knew she must look a mess, but she didn't care. She began to laugh, too, until her eyes grew damp and her sides ached. Gradually, their laughter subsided. Marty felt her heart pounding as Hank closed the distance between them.

"You could have been badly burned. If you had been, it would have been my fault," he said seriously, and reached out a hand to touch her face.

In that instant, Marty felt sure he was going to kiss her again. Though she knew it was wrong, she moved even closer to him. In the space of a heartbeat, she would have been in his arms. But a cool, commanding voice from the doorway said, "I thought we had a date, Hank!"

Chapter Ten

Startled, Marty swung around. A beautiful girl with slender legs in skintight jeans, long ash-blond hair, and a sullen pout was watching them.

"Lila! What are you doing here?" Hank asked, stepping away from Marty.

"I thought you were going to take me to the mall."

Hank shrugged. "I said if we finished up early, I'd try to drop by your house. But as you can see, I'm still working."

Lila looked around the finishing room, an expression of distaste on her pretty face. "But I wanted to show you that necklace I've been telling you about, the one in Jenson's Jewelry Store."

"Sorry, not tonight," Hank said firmly. "Grandpa's sick, so I have to fill in for him."

Lila's razor-sharp gaze flickered over Marty and back to Hank. "Who's your friend?"

Hank flushed. "Sorry—guess I skipped introductions. Lila, this is Marty Evans. She's been helping out today. Marty, this is Lila Downing."

"Nice to meet you," Marty lied.

Lila sniffed, obviously suspicious, and Marty felt guilty over how close she'd come to being in Hank's arms. The exhilaration she had felt only a moment ago had evaporated like steam out of the cupola atop the sugar house roof. She had thought Hank was going to kiss her again, and if it hadn't been for Lila's interruption, she would have let him. What kind of person was she turning into? How could she let herself have these feelings about a guy who belonged to another girl, a guy who wasn't even faithful to that girl?

Marty shivered in her wet shirt. Lila's stylish good looks only served to emphasize her bedraggled state. Eager to escape, she stepped into the storeroom, closed the door and began straightening up the shelves.

"What happened to her, anyway?" she heard Lila ask. "She looks like a drowned rat."

Hank's explanation was spoken so softly that Marty couldn't hear it, but it must have been funny because she heard Lila whoop with laughter.

Angry and embarrassed at being made fun of, Marty swung back toward the door. But she couldn't make herself open it and face Lila's amusement. She heard Hank say, "Marty has worked hard all day. We both have."

Lila made a disgusted noise. "Honestly, Hank! Why don't you apply for a job at one of those shops in the mall? Then you could dress for success instead of messing around in sticky syrup all day long. There's absolutely no future in it."

"How about letting me worry about that?" Hank said, his voice rising.

"Don't yell at me, Hank Maxwell!" Lila snapped.

"Then don't try and tell me what I should and shouldn't do!" Hank snapped back.

Lila sighed loudly. "It seems like all we do lately is argue. And I don't want it to be that way between us," she said, her tone suddenly cajoling. "We can compromise, can't we? If you insist on finishing up here, I'll go home. We can go to the mall tomorrow night instead."

"I thought you had a date with that guy

on the debating team tomorrow night," Hank said.

"I'll break it."

"Why would you want to do that? I thought you wanted to see other guys. You said we should *both* see other people."

"Yes, I did," Lila replied. "That's why you can't make me jealous by working late with that girl."

Marty gasped. Had Hank been trying to get back at Lila by showing interest in her? Had he just been using her? If he had . . . why, the jerk! Furious and humiliated, Marty flung open the door and marched out, startling both of them. "It looks like we're about done here," she said. "I'm going home."

"Wait a second, Marty . . ." Hank began, but she refused to look at him. She grabbed her coat and hurried out of the sugar house.

"Slow down," Hank called after her. "I'll tell Gram you're leaving so she can pay you."

"Tell her to give my check to Brenda. She'll get it to me."

Thankful for the darkness that hid her gathering tears, Marty threw the slicker over her shoulders and ran to the car.

As she turned the car around, the headlights caught Hank in their beams. He lifted his hand in a wave and stepped out of the way. Marty gripped the steering wheel tight and drove on. As her tires sloshed through puddles in the lane, tears trickled down her cheeks. The more she thought about it, the more certain she was that Hank didn't care at all about her! He wasn't worth her tears! Scrubbing her cheeks with the back of her hand, she turned onto the highway. But the tears continued to flow.

In spite of her efforts, Marty couldn't seem to get Hank out of her mind. Sunday was a long, dreary day, and Monday wasn't much of an improvement. Darrin caught up with her after lunch and wanted to know if she'd talked to Brenda about him. Marty was purposely vague, not wanting to give him false hopes.

"Bren likes to play the field—you know how she is," she told him.

"Well, I was looking ahead to the Sweetheart Dance," Darrin said. "If I thought she'd go with me . . ."

"The Sweetheart Dance? That's a month and a half away!"

"I know, but I'm on the planning committee and we're working hard to make it really special this year," Darrin replied. "It'll be held at the lodge at Sunset Falls. The

Drama Club's tech crew is going to set up some special lighting and light up the falls. It should be terrific, all lit up at night. And there'll be a live band, of course, plus catered refreshments."

Marty could see it so clearly—the spacious main room of the lodge with its massive beams high overhead, a crackling fire in the huge stone fireplace, the refreshment table nearby, the wide window looking out on the lighted falls. And the coronation of the Sweetheart Couple. . . . Realizing with a pang that she herself would probably not get to go, she said, "About Brenda—you'll never know if you don't ask."

Frowning, Darrin said, "I thought you agreed to help."

As if she had let him down! "I'm trying," Marty sighed. "What do you want me to do—ask her for you?"

"Well, if you're going to be that way about it . . ." he grumbled, then walked away looking hurt. Marty heaved another sigh. How come the person you liked never seemed to like you? Life could sure be a bummer sometimes!

"You haven't said ten words all day," Brenda commented on the ride home from school that afternoon. "Something wrong?"

"Just thinking about D.C.," Marty said, and it was partly true. She *had* been thinking of D.C., along with everything else that had gone wrong recently.

"Still haven't found him a home, huh?"

"There's one possibility, but things got kind of mixed up, and I don't think anything's going to come of it," Marty said. "Maybe I should run an ad in the paper."

"That's a good idea." Brenda shot her another quick glance and frowned. "You're sure that's all that's bugging you?"

"Well, I'm wondering what I'm going to do with the Phantom Spry tickets, now that Darrin . . ." she began.

"Ask someone else!" Brenda said promptly.

"Like who?"

"How about Hank?"

"I don't think Lila would like that," Marty said pointedly.

Brenda turned her car into Marty's driveway and said with a shrug, "Who cares about Lila? Hank likes Phantom Spry a lot. He just might go."

"I wouldn't want him to do me any favors," Marty said and jumped out of the car before it had rolled to a complete stop.

"Hey! What's eating you?" Brenda asked.

Marty hesitated, sorely tempted to tell her. Though Brenda might suspect her feelings for Hank, Marty had never confessed how much she cared about him, and she wasn't about to do it now. Hugging her books, she hung her head and mumbled, "I'm sorry, Bren. It's been a bad day, that's all."

Still looking doubtful, Brenda said, "Get back in and you can tell me all about it on the way to Party World. I want to pick out some decorations for my Just-for-the-Fun-of-It bash."

"You mean your folks finally caved in?" Marty asked.

Brenda grinned. "I caught them at a weak moment, I guess. It was right after I got an A on my chemistry exam!"

Marty shrugged. A trip to the mall was better than sitting around the house feeling sorry for herself. "Let me drop off my books, and I'll be right back."

She paused on her way out again to pick up D.C. and give him a hug. She had put up some "cat for adoption" notices in some of the local stores, and if someone didn't respond soon, he'd have to go to the animal shelter. D.C. struggled in her arms, trying to get down. She released him with a sigh. "You guys are all alike. Rejection, rejection!"

*　　*　　*

The shopping expedition took longer than Marty had expected. And when she got back, she wished she hadn't gone at all. Her mother told her that Hank had delivered her check, and he'd also taken D.C., assuring Mrs. Evans just as he'd assured Marty that the cat would have a good home. She hadn't even had a chance to say good-bye to her pet! The blues returned, full force.

It didn't help a bit when on Friday upon returning home from school, Marty spotted a realtor's sign in Mr. Coltry's front yard.

"Do you *believe* this?" she wailed to Brenda. "I had to get rid of D.C. because of Mr. Coltry, and how he's selling his house and moving away!"

"That's the pits, all right," Brenda sympathized. Then she brightened. "Hey, here's an idea. Why don't you call her up, explain what happened and ask if she'd mind returning D.C.?"

Marty stared at her blankly. "Who? Who are you talking about?"

"Lila Downing, silly."

Even more confused, Marty said, "But Hank took D.C.—" Marty stopped short as she put two and two together. "You mean it was *Lila*? Hank gave *my* cat to his *girlfriend*?"

Brenda shrugged. "I thought you knew."

Marty's head was spinning as she absorbed the news. Lila Downing had *her* cat, *her* beloved pet! How could Hank do that? He'd only used her to make Lila jealous and now he was using D.C. to get back into the good graces of that stuck-up blond!

Brenda was staring at her, obviously puzzled by Marty's reaction. "So are you going to call her?" she asked. "Her family's number is in the phone book."

Marty paused a moment, trying to figure out what to do. She wasn't going to phone, that was for sure. But she had to take action. Lila Downing didn't look like a cat person to her. She probably didn't know the first thing about caring for D.C.! Coming to a decision, Marty announced, "I'm going after my cat!"

"You mean in person?"

"You bet! Want to come with me?"

Brenda nodded immediately and followed Marty into her house, where they looked up *Downing* in the county telephone directory.

"I'm sure she lives in Blue Meadows," Brenda said. "Good—there's only one Downing there."

"Great!" Marty said grimly. "Can we take your car?"

Brenda's face fell. "Mom's got it. What about your dad's car?"

"He's using it, and Mom's at the store." Marty sighed.

"Then how are we going to get to Lila's house?"

Marty flung herself down on the sofa. "I guess we'll have to wait until tomorrow then."

"You *could* call," Brenda suggested again.

Marty shook her head. "I don't want to give Lila too much time to think it over. She doesn't like me."

Brenda looked at her in surprise. "I didn't know you two had met."

"She came out to the camp last Saturday night when Hank and I were working," Marty said.

"Hank! That's an idea," Brenda cried. "Let's call him and have *him* ask Lila to give D.C. back!"

A wave of panic went through Marty. "No! We're not going to do that!"

"But I thought you and Hank were pals. Now you're acting as if . . ." Brenda's look of bewilderment slowly changed to suspicion, then comprehension. "Oooh, I get it! You're in love with Hank! How come you didn't tell me?"

"Because—well, because I hated to admit it when he obviously doesn't feel the same way about me," Marty said miserably. Then she went into a little more detail about the previous Saturday night, telling Brenda how her shirttail had caught on fire and how Hank had just doused the flames when Lila walked in. "You should have seen the way she looked at me when Hank introduced us," she finished.

Brenda rolled her eyes. "So that's what's been bugging you! And all this time I thought you were having second thoughts about breaking up with Darrin and saying you didn't care if I went out with him! This afternoon when he asked me to the Sweetheart Dance, I didn't know what to say. I was worried you'd be upset."

"I hope you're going to say yes," Marty said.

Brenda giggled. "I sure will!" She flung her arms around Marty and gave her a hug. "You should have told me how you felt about Hank!"

"Well, I've told you now," Marty sighed. "Not that it makes any difference. Lila's got Hank—and she's also got my cat!" She scowled. "I may not be able to do anything about Hank, but I'm not letting her keep D.C.!"

"We'll get him back tomorrow," Brenda assured her. "Now I'd better go home. I promised Mom I'd clean my room this afternoon, and if I don't, she just might change her mind about the party!"

Chapter Eleven

"Turn down that alley," Brenda ordered.

Perspiring in her heavy oilskin slicker, Marty did as she was told. "Shouldn't we just go to the door and ask?"

"You really think Lila's going to give him up without a fight? Fat chance! Not if she caught you and Hank together at the sugar house making eyes at each other."

"We were *not* making eyes . . ." Marty began indignantly.

"Whatever," Brenda said with an impatient flick of her hand. Pulling her hat down to shadow her face, she opened the car door and climbed out. The hat and the long black trench coat she was wearing made her look like a cartoon spy.

"Where are you going?" Marty asked.

"If we're lucky, D.C. will be outside. Simple to snatch," said Brenda cheerfully. "Keep the motor running!"

Marty was so nervous she felt sick. Her pulse hammered in her throat as she watched Brenda sneak down the alley. This was one of Brenda's crazy schemes, and she knew she shouldn't allow her to do it. Of course, D.C. *was* her cat. Or at least, he used to be her cat. She jumped out and raced after her friend, calling, "Wait up! I'm coming too!"

Brenda touched a finger to her lips in warning. They crept up the alley, then stepped behind a tall hedge that bordered Lila's spacious backyard.

"It *is* as big as a football field," Marty whispered.

"Shhh!"

The hedge was too thick for them to pass through, so Marty got down on her stomach and pulled aside prickly branches until she made a space big enough to see through. Brenda found a slightly larger gap in the bushes. Marty watched breathlessly as Brenda wiggled and squirmed, poking first her head, then her shoulders through the hole. All at once Brenda hissed, "There he is!"

"D.C.?" Marty whispered. "Are you sure it's him?"

"Sure I'm sure. He's black, he's wearing a rhinestone collar, and he's crouched beneath a bird feeder!"

Marty nodded. "Sounds like D.C., all right."

"Here, kitty, kitty. Here, D.C.!" Brenda called softly.

Marty began calling, too. She peered through her own small hole, but she still couldn't see her cat.

"He's coming," Brenda cried. "Marty, he's coming!" She wormed her way further through the hedge and whispered, "He's coming closer. A few more inches—I'm touching fur!"

Through her peek hole, Marty suddenly spotted two pairs of legs, two pairs of feet. "Bren, look out! Someone's coming!"

Marty's throat went dry as a pair of heavy overshoes and a pair of black leather high-heeled boots marched across the grass toward the hedge. "We've got to get out of here!" she cried.

"I've got him! Quick, Marty! Let's beat it!" Brenda shouted.

Marty started to sprint to the car, but her legs felt as heavy as lead and she seemed to be running in slow motion. At last she got inside and flung open the passenger door. Brenda threw herself in, clutching D.C.

"Put the pedal to the metal!" Brenda yelled.

Marty floored the accelerator, but nothing happened. The motor was running but the car wouldn't move! Through the windshield, she saw a tall form loping toward them up the alley. It was Hank, with Lila close behind, her ash-blond hair streaming in the breeze.

Marty cringed as Hank reached through the open car window and snatched her fedora from her head.

"Desperado!" he shouted. But there was no tenderness in his voice and no gentle laughter. "Catnapper!" His big hands closed over her shoulders, shaking her, Shaking her hard . . .

"Marty? Wake up, Marty. I'm home."

Marty sat up with a jerk. It was her mother touching her shoulder, not Hank. Her heart was pounding so hard that her chest hurt. She took a deep breath and rubbed her eyes.

"Did I startle you? I'm sorry, honey," her mother said.

Marty shuddered. "I was having the most awful dream! Brenda and I cat-snatched D.C.! When I saw the sign in Mr. Coltry's yard, I thought I might try to get him back. But after that dream . . ." She shook her head sadly. "It wouldn't be right. A deal's a deal.

D.C.'s gone for good and I might as well get used to it."

Trying very hard not to think about either D.C. or Hank, Marty got along one day at a time. As for Brenda, all she could talk about was the party she was giving.

"I told Hank to stop by, but I doubt that he will," she told Marty one day on the ride home from school.

"Why not?" Marty asked, alarmed at how her heart raced at the mere mention of his name.

Brenda slowed for a stop light. "He said he wouldn't know anyone. Different school, stuff like that."

"He'd know you."

Brenda grinned. "Yeah, but I don't think he'd get very excited about dancing with his cousin. So I told him you'd be there. . . ."

"You didn't!" Marty groaned.

Brenda glanced at her. "Sure I did. But he thinks you're mad at him or something because you haven't been out to the camp lately."

Marty's shoulders slumped. "He's got Lila. Why should he care if I'm mad at him or not? I don't go out there anymore because it hurts me too much to know that he doesn't care about me at all."

"Well, I didn't want to give *that* away, so I told him it was just because you've been busy," Brenda told her.

Wishing Hank's name had never come up, Marty said, "Let's just forget it, okay? I know he's your cousin, but I don't want to talk about him. I don't even want to *think* about him anymore."

But it seemed the harder Marty tried to forget Hank, the more frequently he came to mind. The syrup she poured on her pancakes, old pickup trucks, and jigsaw puzzles all reminded her of him. Even Mr. Coltry's bird feeder made her think of Hank, and each time she thought of him, her heart ached. He had seemed like such a nice, sensitive guy—at first, anyway.

On the Friday before Brenda's party there was no school, but Brenda turned up at the Evanses' house at the usual time anyway. "What are you up to today?" she asked, bouncing into Marty's room.

Still in bed, Marty pushed tangled tresses back from her face and yawned. "I *was* sleeping in. Teachers' Convention, remember?" Marty rubbed the sleep from her eyes. "So what are *you* up to?"

"I'm going out to Gram's. Thought maybe you'd like to go along."

"No, thanks," Marty murmured.

Brenda sat on the edge of her bed. "Hank'll be there."

Marty raised her eyebrows. "Hank who?"

Brenda scowled. "Would you quit being so stubborn and give a little?"

"And have him think I'm chasing after him? No thanks! Lila Downing can have him."

Brenda heaved a huge sigh. "If you won't cooperate, what can I do?"

"You *could* let me go back to sleep," Marty said hopefully.

Brenda rolled her eyes and changed the subject. "I invited Darrin to the party. I figured if we're going to the Sweetheart Dance together, we ought to get in a little groundwork. He said he'd come."

"That's nice," Marty said.

Brenda shot her a sidelong glance. "You're sure you don't mind?"

"For the hundredth time, *I don't mind.* You'll be good for each other," Marty said. But inwardly, she was worrying about tomorrow night. What if she was the only one there without a date? And looking even further ahead, what about the Sweetheart Dance? She probably wouldn't have a date for it either. One thing about Darrin—he'd always been there. Though she didn't regret breaking up with him, not having a steady guy had its down side.

As the hour of the party approached, Marty's nervousness increased. The last few parties she'd been to, Darrin had been by her side. Not that they spent every moment together, but she'd never had to worry whether anyone would ask her to dance or who she'd talk to when everyone paired off. Tonight would be different.

Marty changed her outfit three times before deciding on a black jumpsuit. It had three-quarter-length sleeves and full trousers that tapered to snug bands at the ankles. Gold earrings and black flats completed the ensemble.

Standing in front of her mirror, Marty checked out the effect of a comb with a black silk flower holding her blond hair back on one side. She decided she liked it, and took pains with the curling iron, shaping her blunt cut into soft waves.

"What do you think?" Marty asked her parents when she came into the living room.

Her mother smiled. "You look terrific! I don't know why you're feeling so anxious. You always have a good time at Brenda's."

But this is different, Marty thought as her

father kissed her cheek and followed her mother into the kitchen. Alone with her jitters, Marty paced back and forth, then crossed to the window. Cars were arriving next door. Everyone was coming in pairs, like the animals in Noah's Ark. Should she go at all? Maybe it would be safer just to stay home.

But Marty raised her chin. She believed in women's lib, didn't she? Who said she needed a date to have a good time at her best friend's party? She'd go, and she'd have fun if it killed her!

A breathless Brenda met her at the door. "You're late!"

"It's a long commute," Marty joked.

Marty glanced across the room and spotted the pretty, raven-haired foreign exchange student. As usual, she was surrounded by boys.

"She's been flirting with Darrin ever since she got here." Brenda wrinkled her nose. "I only invited her in the interest of international good will."

Marty giggled. "Who are you kidding? You just wanted to get all the guys here!"

Brenda gave her a shameless grin. "Worked, too, didn't it? Three guys for every two girls. Count 'em!" Then she excused herself, saying, "I've gotta put in a new disc. Have a seat there by the lake," she added, pointing to a round blue area rug.

Inventive when it came to decorations, Brenda had outdone herself tonight, using cardboard carpet rolls and green construction paper to make trees, which stood on either side of a white latticework arbor. Beneath the arbor was a bench, facing the blue rug "lake." Marty had no sooner seated herself when Brenda's younger brother, Patrick, plopped down beside her and stretched one shoe toward the rug. "Look! I'm getting my foot wet!"

Marty laughed and touched the rug with her toe. "So am I!"

Just as she did, Brenda hopped up on a stool and announced over the din, "Marty's our first Lady of the Lake! Stay right where you are, Marty—you too, Patrick. Patrick's our pot of gold. Okay, this is a dollar dance! You guys line up and drop a dollar into the pot of gold to dance with our Lady of the Lake."

Marty's cheeks burned as a few of the boys shifted from foot to foot, looking uncertain. Each second seemed like an eternity. *What if no one stepped forward?* This was definitely not one of Brenda's better ideas!

Brenda went on, "In case you're wondering, we're going to order pizzas and soda with the money. So if you're hungry, thirsty, or just want to get this party rolling, line up and start dancing!"

Chapter Twelve

Marty was beginning to wish she could drown in the "lake" when Darrin strode up and gave Patrick a dollar. For a moment, when he smiled and took Marty in his arms, it almost seemed like old times. But as they danced, Marty knew that the spark between them had burned out. One hand in his, the other on his shoulder, she wondered what it would be like to be held this way by Hank. But just as the thought surfaced, she squelched it.

"Great party, isn't it?" Darrin said.

Marty smiled. "You can always count on Bren for something original."

"I know. Isn't she terrific?"

Noting his goofy expression, Marty chuckled to herself and agreed, "She sure is."

Then Todd Williams cut in. They had danced no more than a minute or two when there was another cut, then another. By the time the music stopped, Marty had danced with every boy in the room.

Brenda counted the cash, then dethroned Marty and proclaimed Darrin Lord of the Lake. All the girls giggled, lined up, and passed their dollars to Patrick.

Patrick handled the cash flow while Brenda went to the phone to order the pizza. The doorbell kept ringing, kids kept arriving and by the time the pizzas arrived, the Kellys' family room was overflowing with teens talking and dancing and having a wonderful time. To her surprise, Marty had a good time, too.

Brenda's party was the talk of Riverton High for the first few days of the following week. Some of the guys Marty had danced with smiled and spoke to her as they passed her in the halls. The week before, the same guys hadn't known she was alive.

"Just one of the perks of having a weird friend who throws great parties!" Marty said, as she and Brenda ate lunch together on Wednesday.

"Who're you calling weird?" Brenda laughed. "Anyway, you're underestimating yourself.

They're paying attention to you because they're interested. Follow the advice you gave me about Darrin—give 'em a little encouragement! You've still got that extra concert ticket. Use it!"

"The concert's the day after tomorrow. It's kind of late to be asking someone now," Marty said.

"So you're just going to waste it?"

"Why don't you take it?" Marty suggested. "Maybe Patrick would like to go."

Brenda said. "I don't think Roger would be exactly thrilled to drag my kid brother along. But if you're really not going to ask anyone else, I'll see if he wants to go."

As Marty dug through her pocketbook for the extra Phantom Spry ticket, Brenda added. "Why don't you ride along with Roger and me? Half the fun of a concert is going with friends."

Thinking aloud, Marty said. "We won't be able to sit together. The tickets are all reserved, and I bought mine long after you did."

"I know, but at least we can share a ride there," Brenda said. "The fewer cars, the better. The traffic's bound to be awful, especially when the concert lets out."

Marty agreed it was a good idea.

"By the way, I know a secret," Brenda said.

Her cheeks were pink and her eyes were twinkling with excitement. "It's about the Sweetheart Dance, and you have to promise, cross your heart and hope to die, that you won't tell a single soul!"

"Deal," Marty said, crossing her heart. "Spill it."

Brenda leaned closer to her. "There was a student council meeting last night, and . . ." she glanced around, then whispered in Marty's ear, "they've nominated the Sweetheart candidates! Darrin's one of them, and if he wins . . ."

"You two will be the Sweetheart Couple!" Marty finished for her. Each year Riverton High's student council chose two boys and two girls as candidates. The student body voted by secret ballot, and the results of the election were announced at the dance. The winner and his or her date were crowned the Sweetheart Couple.

Brenda laid a hand on Marty's arm and said, "I'm thrilled, but I can't help feeling a little guilty, too. I mean, if you and Darrin hadn't broken up . . ."

"Forget it," Marty said, smiling. "I'm happy for you, Bren, really I am."

Brenda gave her an impulsive hug. "What did I do to rate such a terrific best friend?"

"Luck of the Irish, I guess," Marty said with a grin. "Now if only some of that luck would rub off on me. I'd hate to miss that dance."

"There's plenty of time, Marty. Somebody will ask you, you'll see," Brenda told her. But to Marty, it sounded like wishful thinking.

The night of the concert was unseasonably mild, so Marty decided to wear her denim miniskirt. It was so soft from many washings and so faded that it nearly matched the long-sleeved chambray shirt she slipped on over her red tank top. As she dressed, Marty thought about the Sweetheart Dance. During gym class, several girls had asked Marty if she was going, and she had to admit that she didn't have a date yet. Most of her friends already had dates lined up, and she knew they felt sorry for her.

Forget it, she ordered herself. Tonight, just for a few hours, she was going to concentrate on nothing but the music.

A horn honked in the driveway, and Marty ran down the stairs.

"Have a good time!" her mother called as she hurried through the living room. Her father gave her a hug and folded a few extra dollars into her hand.

"In case of an emergency," he said. Marty thanked him with a kiss and dashed out the door.

Roger, Brenda's date, got out of the car and held the door open for her. The back seat was empty.

"Isn't Patrick coming?" Marty asked as she climbed in.

Brenda shook her head. "Nope. He opted for a Disney double feature instead."

"Stood up by an eight-year-old! Now that's hitting bottom," Marty complained.

Roger joined in the laughter. Marty was relieved that he didn't seem to mind her horning in on his date with Brenda. Brenda turned around in her seat, including Marty in the conversation as they drove to the Assembly Hall.

Even though they were early, mobs of people were already filing into the auditorium. Brenda and Roger's seats were two sections away from Marty's. After they bought concert posters, they agreed on a place to meet during intermission, then went their separate ways.

Marty found her seat and sat back, watching the huge auditorium fill around her. By the time the lights came down, the seat to her left seemed to be the only empty one in the entire place. Marty kept telling herself that she didn't mind not having a date. She'd managed just fine at Brenda's party, and she'd enjoy herself tonight, too. She wasn't lonely, not the least little bit. At least, she wouldn't be once the music began.

Marty had never heard of the band that opened for Phantom Spry, but they had a great sound. She clapped and cheered with the rest of the crowd as they finished their last song.

There was a moment's delay after the group made their exit. Then suddenly a thick mist filled the stage and an eerie light shone on it. Phantom Spry's lead singer leaped out of the dense fog, striking a chord on his guitar. The band burst into their opening number, accompanied by a stunning light show. As the last notes faded, Marty leaped to her feet, joining the thunderous applause.

The lights on stage went out again, hushing the crowd, and everyone sat down. The music picked up tempo and volume and kept building and building until it reached a crashing crescendo.

Caught up in the magic of the special effects, Marty didn't notice when someone stopped in the aisle beside her seat. Keeping her eyes glued on the stage, she moved her knees to one side to let the person pass. She didn't even turn her head when he sat down in the empty seat next to hers.

"Sorry I'm late. Bronco Betty quit on me," Hank said, leaning close to be heard above the music.

Marty felt as though she'd just had an electric shock. She stared at him in disbelief. It was not a dream. Hank Maxwell was really sitting in the seat beside her.

He leaned even closer, his lips brushing her ear, his arm nudging hers on the arm rest. "Thanks a lot for the ticket. I really wanted to see these guys!"

Marty could scarcely hear the music over the rapid pounding of her heart.

Chapter Thirteen

Brenda! Marty thought. Her impulsive, well-intentioned, meddling best friend had given the extra ticket to Hank! She couldn't think of a single thing to say.

Hank reached for her hand. "Great music, isn't it?" he shouted in her ear.

She nodded wordlessly, thankful that the volume of the music and the cheers of the audience made conversation nearly impossible.

Marty was keenly aware of his touch. It was tempting to shove aside all her doubts and confusion and live only for the moment, but there were too many unanswered questions. Lila was the biggest question of all. Had they broken up? Or was Hank just "seeing other people" while still hanging onto his relationship with Lila? Was that why he was here, holding her hand?

When the song ended, Marty withdrew her hand to applaud, and Hank did not reach for it again. Marty told herself that it was for the best, at least until she knew where she stood with him. What would she say to him at intermission? What would *he* say to *her*?

"How about a soda?" Hank asked as the house lights came on.

Marty nodded numbly.

"Do you want to stay here, or come with me?" Hank asked.

Struggling to regain her composure, Marty said, "I may as well come. I told Brenda I'd meet her during intermission."

She followed him into the crowded aisle, up the steps and into the lobby. They found Brenda standing next to a column near the concession stand. Grinning from ear to ear, she said, "What do you think of the show?"

"Those guys are great." Marty kept her tone light and casual, but the look she sent Brenda was something else.

Brenda batted innocent eyes and declared, "They're the best! Especially the lead guitarist. Is he gorgeous or what?"

Hank glanced around. "Where's your date?" he asked her.

"Roger's getting us something to drink."

"Guess I better get in line, too. Be back in a minute," Hank said.

Brenda's eyes twinkled as he started away. "Surprised?" she asked Marty the minute they were alone.

Marty clutched Brenda's arm. "Boy, do you have a lot of explaining to do! I nearly fainted when Hank sat down next to me! What did you tell him to get him here? Where's Lila? Does she know about this?"

Brenda just kept grinning. "What does it matter? He came, didn't he?"

"Bren, I'm *dying* here!" Marty wailed. "I don't know how to act!"

"Just be yourself," Brenda advised with a smirk.

"Easy for you to say!" Marty retorted. "I've got to know what *he* thinks this is! I mean, he's here and I'm here, but it isn't a date, and if it isn't a date, what *is* it? *What did you tell him?*"

"Just that you had an extra ticket, and that you mentioned . . . hey! Isn't that Rochelle Hosier?"

Not about to be distracted, Marty tightened her grip on Brenda's arm. "Tell me *word for word* what you said when you offered Hank the ticket!"

Brenda rolled her eyes. "Okay, okay! Don't break my arm! First, I told him you had this extra ticket. He wanted to know if it was your idea for him to use it, and I could see he wasn't going to take it if I told him you didn't know. So I . . . well, I kinda fibbed and said you wanted him to have it, and you'd meet him here."

"So he's under the impression *I* asked *him* out when I knew he was dating someone else?" Marty groaned. "Bren, how could you *do* that? He must think I have tons of nerve!"

"Hey, he's here, isn't he?" Brenda said cheerfully.

"Yeah, but probably just to hear Phantom Spry."

"Would you stop it!" Brenda exclaimed. "Here's your opportunity! I bet when Hank takes you home, he'll ask you out."

"Takes me home?" Marty echoed. "How do you know he's taking me home? Does *he* know he's taking me home?"

"Of course he does. He's your date, isn't he?"

"No! Yes—I don't know!" Marty wailed. "What about Lila? Are they still seeing each other?"

"Search me. Hank didn't say." Brenda dashed off, calling back, "There's Roger with our drinks. See you later!"

"Bren! Wait a minute!"

But Brenda kept right on going.

"One of these days, Brenda Kelly!" Marty muttered under her breath.

"Something wrong?"

Marty spun around to find Hank at her elbow. "No! No, everything's fine," she said quickly.

"Here's your drink." Hank passed her a soda, then took a sip of his own. His brown eyes searched her face. "You sure nothing's wrong? You look upset."

"No, I'm fine. Really!" Marty flashed a strained smile.

"Okay, if you're sure. By the way, I told Roger not to wait for you, that I'd take you home. Is that okay?"

"That's fine," Marty murmured. *I sound like a broken record*, she thought.

He smiled down at her and finished his drink. "Let's find our seats before they dim the lights."

They put their empty cups in a waste container. Then Marty silently led the way back to their seats.

Phantom Spry once again took the stage by storm. The special effects were no less spectacular than those in the early part of the show, but Marty was so distracted by Hank's nearness that she could concentrate on nothing else.

Near the end of the show, the band led into "Don't Let 'Em Say You Can't." Hank nudged her. "That's your song, right?"

Marty nodded, sitting perfectly still as the familiar lyrics filled the auditorium. In the darkness, Hank reached for Marty's hand. A wave of pleasure swept over her. Content for the moment to relish his touch, she wished the music could go on forever. But of course it didn't. All too soon, the last notes of the final song faded, the cheers and applause died away, and the auditorium began emptying.

"Let's stop and get a T-shirt," Hank said as they inched along the crowded aisle. By the time they got to the stand where the shirts were sold, there were only a few left. Hank bought one, then handed it to Marty.

"You keep it," she protested.

He held it up to his wide shoulders. "Kind of small for me, don't you think?" He folded it again and gave it to her.

Still confused, but aglow inside and out, Marty smiled and thanked him.

"Thank *you* for the ticket," Hank said as

they went out of the building. "I had a great time."

"Me, too," Marty murmured. After the stuffiness of the auditorium, the cool night air was a pleasant contrast. "I'm really glad you could come," she added.

"Are you kidding? I wouldn't have missed it for the world!" Hank said, tucking her arm in his. They crossed the busy street and started walking through the first of several parking lots. He smiled down at Marty. "When Brenda said that you were coming with her, I was kind of disappointed you wouldn't be riding with me. But it worked out for the best, I guess, since the truck broke down. I would have hated it if I'd made you late too."

"But if Bronco Betty broke down, what are we going home in?" Marty asked.

"I hoofed it to a neighbor's and called Dad," Hank told her as they wove their way through another parking lot. "He picked me up in his car, I drove him home, and came straight here. Did you think I wasn't coming?"

"Well . . ." Marty hesitated and he waited for her to go on. She drew a deep breath and plunged in. "To tell you the truth, I didn't *know* you were coming."

"What do you mean, you didn't know?"

By the headlamps of an oncoming car,

Marty saw the puzzled expression on his face. Hoping she wasn't ruining everything, she admitted in a small voice, "I didn't know Bren gave you the ticket."

"But she said . . ." Hank let go of her arm. After what seemed to Marty like a very long silence, he said. "This was all Brenda's doing, wasn't it? I should have known!" He shot Marty a disconcerted glance. "I'll bet she heard Lila and I broke up and decided to take matters into her own hands." He shoved his fists into his pockets. "You must think I'm a real jerk, taking that ticket when you didn't even know . . . I'll pay you for it."

Marty ignored the money he thrust at her. "You broke up?" she echoed. At his nod, she felt a surge of joy. "When?"

Hank stopped beneath a street lamp and shoved his hands into the pockets of his jeans. A slow flush spread up his neck to his face as he stared at his feet. "Lila told me about a month ago she wanted to date other people. She said I should too, but at the time, I didn't think I wanted to. What I mean is . . ." He paused and raked a hand through his hair. "Well, we'd been quarreling a lot, but I figured if we stuck it out . . ." He broke off again, and looked directly at Marty. "Then I met you, and I began to realize Lila and I really had outgrown each other. The reason we kept fighting all the time was . . . well, when it came right down to it, we weren't right for each other."

"And then?" Marty prompted.

"Well, Lila kind of wanted it both ways. She almost convinced me we could date each other and see other people, too." Hank dug his hands deeper into his pockets and ducked his head. "The night we went sledding, I was kind of thinking that way. But then when I kissed you, it got kind of confusing—I mean, I knew I liked you very much, but at the same time, I felt disloyal to Lila."

"But if she was the one who wanted . . ."

"Yeah, I know. That's what I kept telling myself, but it just didn't feel right. Then that night in the sugar house when you caught fire, I finally admitted to myself it was *you* I cared about, not Lila."

"But you took my cat and gave him to *her*," Marty murmured.

Hank raised his head. Looking genuinely surprised, he said, "I thought that was what you wanted—a good home for D.C. I was just trying to help you out."

Marty's heart lurched with rekindled hope. "But why didn't you call me? Or come by? I mean, if you felt that way . . ."

"I didn't think I stood a chance," he mumbled. "Not after Brenda's party."

Marty stared at him. "You were there?"

Hank nodded. "I stuck my head in for a few minutes. Every guy there was dancing with you, so I figured I might as well give up. What chance did I have against all that competition?"

The dollar dance! Marty opened her mouth to explain, but before she could, he said, "That's why, when Brenda gave me that ticket and said you wanted me to meet you at the concert, I couldn't believe it. I mean, all those guys and you were asking *me*! Except you weren't," he said sadly.

"But I would have," Marty said softly, "if I'd known you'd come. But you were going steady with Lila—or I thought you were—and I knew I couldn't possibly compete with *her*, so . . ."

As Hank began to smile, Marty held out a tentative hand. He took it in both of his and squeezed it tight.

"Lila can't compete with *you*," he said gruffly. "We never did have much in common. She was always trying to turn me into something I'm not. But you—well, you made me feel good about myself. Tell you the truth, I think Lila was kind of relieved when I told her I thought we ought to break up. But she made a big scene anyway. She returned everything I ever gave her." He paused, looking sheepish. "Including D.C."

Marty's mouth dropped open. "*You've* got my cat?"

Hank nodded. "I didn't know what else to do with him." Looking uncomfortable, he added, "I don't suppose your father has had second thoughts?"

"You mean I can have him back?" Marty cried. "Oh, Hank! That's wonderful! Thank you! Thank you so much!"

Hank pulled her close, and Marty's heart sang a glorious song as his lips brushed hers.

"I've been wanting to do this again ever since we went sledding," he said softly.

"Me, too," Marty admitted. "I tried to forget about that night, but I just couldn't."

His cheek against hers, Hank said, "When you stopped coming out to the camp, I was afraid I'd never see you again. I thought you must be mad at me."

"I wasn't." Marty closed her eyes as their lips met in another sweet, lingering kiss.

Even when the kiss had ended, Hank kept his arms around her. "Bren mentioned that there's a dance coming up at Riverton High," he said. "If you haven't already made plans . . ."

"I haven't," Marty said breathlessly.

Hank's arms tightened around her. "That's terrific!" He looked down at her tenderly. "Would you want to go with me?"

Would she want to! It was a dream come true! Pulse pounding wildly, Marty whispered, "I'd love to!"

She raised her face to his, knowing as she returned his kiss that she was the happiest—and the luckiest—girl in the world.

SWEET DREAMS are fresh, fun and exciting—
alive with the flavor of the contemporary teen
scene—the joy and doubt of first love. If you've
missed any SWEET DREAMS titles, then you're
missing out on your kind of stories, written about
people like you!

☐	26976-3	**P.S. I LOVE YOU #1** Barbara P. Conklin	$2.99
☐	28633-1	**LOVE ON STRIKE #174** J. Boies	$2.75
☐	28830-X	**PUPPY LOVE #175** Carla Bracale	$2.95
☐	28840-7	**WRONG-WAY ROMANCE #176** Sherri Cobb	$2.95
☐	28862-8	**THE TRUTH ABOUT LOVE #177** Laurie Lykken	$2.95
☐	28900-4	**PROJECT BOYFRIEND #178** Stephanie St. Pierre	$2.95
☐	28962-4	**RACING HEARTS #179** Susan Sloate	$2.99
☐	29021-5	**OPPOSITES ATTRACT #180** Linda Joy Singleton	$2.99
☐	29059-2	**TIME OUT FOR LOVE #181** June O'Connell	$2.99
☐	29144-0	**DOWN WITH LOVE #182** Carla Bracale	$2.99